"Meet Me Here Tomorrow, And I'll Take You For A Ride."

"A ... ride?" She eyed the big black motorcycle warily.

Reno folded his arms and tilted his head back, teasing Jenna with his lazy drawl and self-confident smile. "Come on, Gingerbread Lady, if I didn't gobble you up tonight when I had the chance, what do you think's gonna happen in broad daylight?"

"All right, all right!" She surrendered, feeling as breathless and scared as a child on a Ferris wheel.

The mocking grin, boyishly cleft chin and sorcerer's eyes abruptly disappeared, eclipsed by a dark mirrored visor. As magically as a wizard changing his physical form, he became the warrior again, the awesome black knight, pulling on his gauntlets.

Then he touched a gloved finger to his helmet and roared away into the night.

Dear Reader:

Welcome to Silhouette Desire—sensual, compelling, believable love stories written by and for today's woman. When you open the pages of a Silhouette Desire, you open yourself up to a whole new world— a world of promising passion and endless love.

Each and every Silhouette Desire is a wonderful love story that is both sensuous *and* emotional. You're with the hero and heroine each and every step of the way—from their first meeting, to their first kiss... to their happy ending. You'll experience all the deep joys—and occasional tribulations—of falling in love.

In future months, look for Silhouette Desire novels from some of your favorite authors, such as Naomi Horton, Nancy Martin, Linda Lael Miller and Lass Small, just to name a few.

So go wild with Desire. You'll be glad you did!

Lucia Macro
Senior Editor

KATHLEEN CREIGHTON

THE HEART MENDER

SILHOUETTE *Desire*

Published by Silhouette Books New York

America's Publisher of Contemporary Romance

SILHOUETTE BOOKS
300 East 42nd St., New York, N.Y. 10017

ISBN: 0-373-05584-6

First Silhouette Books printing August 1990

Books by Kathleen Creighton

Silhouette Intimate Moments

Demon Lover #84
Double Dealings #157
Gypsy Dancer #196
In Defense of Love #216
Rogue's Valley #240
Tiger Dawn #289
Love and Other Surprises #322

Silhouette Desire

The Heart Mender #584

KATHLEEN CREIGHTON

has roots deep in the California soil and still lives in the valley where her mother and grandmother were born. As a child, she enjoyed listening to old timers' tales, and her fascination with the past only deepened as she grew older. Today, she says she is interested in everything—art, music, gardening, zoology, anthropology and history, but people are at the top of her list. She also has a lifelong passion for writing, and now combines her two loves into romance novels.

One

There were thirteen Harley-Davidsons parked in front of the old stagecoach station. Jenna McBride sat in her car with the windows rolled up and the doors prudently locked and counted them again. Yep, thirteen.

She thought, Maybe I don't need a cup of coffee all that badly.

But she went on staring at the bikes and the old coach station, finding something about the scene strangely compelling—the weathered log building backed up against the canyon wall like a beleaguered beetle making a last brave stand against the giant warrior ants the motorcycles so strongly resembled. It was symbolic, she thought. A relic of a slower, simpler time holding the machine age at bay. The artist in her found the incongruity irresistible; the romantic found the symbolism poignant, even sad.

She'd seen the sign for the old coach station any number of times while speeding north on the highway that cut through the coastal mountains and into the valley. Though it had intrigued her, she'd always been too intent on going somewhere else to stop and investigate, and had passed it by, saying to herself, *Someday* . . .

But today she'd encountered heavy traffic heading out of L.A., and then freeway construction in Santa Barbara. The blacktop ribbon had begun to uncoil endlessly before her like a hypnotist's spiral. The little sign on the edge of the gorge had seemed like a signal, a snap of the fingers, releasing her from the grip of a spell.

OLD COACH STATION INN, 1 mile.

There would be coffee there, she thought. She could kill two birds with one stone—satisfy her curiosity and at the same time fortify herself for the remainder of the long drive. Nancy was expecting her for dinner, but she could call and let her know she was running late. There would almost certainly be a pay phone at the inn.

So it was a spur-of-the-moment thing, the decision to turn left and follow the sign and its arrow down into the gorge instead of soaring over it as she usually did, on a breathtaking span of steel and concrete. And as the narrow, winding road carried her deeper into the canyon she somehow felt as if she were leaving that world behind her—the world of man-made marvels and machines and deadlines—and entering another where life was simpler, if not gentler, and moved at a less frantic pace.

At four o'clock on a mid-March afternoon it was already approaching twilight in the gorge, and under the newly budding sycamores, the shadows were purple and deep and the birdsong hushed. The air was cool and smelled of new grass and damp earth and moss. It seemed to Jenna a timeless, mythical place. An enchanted place. From somewhere in the deepest recesses of her memory came a name, shrouded in rosy, romantic mists: *Avalon*. Yes, that was it— the forests of Avalon. Where had she heard that? She couldn't remember, but for some reason it conjured up visions of medieval knights, fairy queens and unicorns.

While lost in that misty daydream she'd rounded a bend and come at last upon the old stagecoach station—and the motorcycles.

So much for romance, she thought. The Old Coach Station was obviously a bikers' hangout. Now what? Her first impulse was to start up the car again and keep right on going.

But she told herself she was being unnecessarily timid. Lots of perfectly nice, normal people rode motorcycles; they weren't all hulking, bearded brutes festooned with militant insignias and tattoos. And besides, it was four o'clock in the afternoon and this was a public inn. She'd been driving a long time, and she really did need a break—a bathroom, a telephone, a cup of coffee, a chance to stretch her legs.

Of course, only a few short weeks ago she probably would have disregarded all those rationalizations, taken the prudent course and continued on to the nearest town with a familiar franchise coffee shop or fast-food drive-in. Jenna wasn't a risk taker. She didn't like surprises. She wanted to know how the movie ended before she plunked down money for a ticket.

But a lot had happened to her in those weeks. She'd just taken hold of her emotions and turned them inside out, a procedure no less painful, she was sure, than if someone had performed the same operation on her body. In the vast ache left within her now, there was very little room for fear. Anxiety seemed superfluous to her. Anger and pain, she'd discovered, do breed a certain recklessness.

For one more moment, though, she stood in the protected V of car and door, one hand resting on the roof of the rented Chevy. It wasn't fear that made her hesitate, but something else, something that made her heart beat faster and her nerves quicken, an awareness she could neither name nor explain. There was something about the place....

Except that there was really nothing about the old inn— or even the motorcycles—to foster either anticipation or dread. It was almost unnaturally quiet; except for distant birdsong and the rush of water in the creek across the road, there were no sounds at all. The bikes awaited their riders in expectant silence. The buildings huddled in the purple dusk, their small, deeply recessed windows obscured by signs advertising familiar brands of beer, giving them a blind, secretive look, like mirrored sunglasses.

"Ridiculous," Jenna muttered as she slammed the car door, ruthlessly throttling the colorful imagination with which she'd been both gifted and cursed.

Skirting the Harleys with a firm and confident step, she mounted the split-log steps, pausing to read a poster that was tacked to the heavy plank door before she pushed it open. The poster announced forthcoming appearances by a country-western band. She found something in that promise of live music reassuring.

When she entered the bar, the hum of conversation didn't exactly die, it retreated, making it seem for a moment as if she'd carried a wave of silence into the place with her. Just for a moment, and then the sound came flooding back—low voices and heavy laughter, the scrape of boots on rough wooden planks.

The room was small, dark and murky with cigarette smoke, an authentically rustic rectangle with the entrance and bar centrally placed opposite each other on the long sides. The walls were of thick logs, unadorned except for the usual beer ads and a dart board at one end. The area to the left of the door appeared to be occupied solely by microphones, music stands and miscellaneous sound equipment, as discordant in that setting as the motorcycles outside. The bar's customers were gathered around small wooden tables at the other end of the rectangle. Without actually looking that way, Jenna was aware of large bodies huddled in the gloom, of black leather and blue denim and masculinity, and of an invisible but unmistakable current of quickening interest.

She focused on the lighted bar and made a beeline for it.

"Can I help you?" the bartender asked doubtfully as she hitched herself onto a stool at the unoccupied end of the bar. He had a taciturn, watchful manner that reminded Jenna of a saloon keeper in an old Western. He looked as if he'd be ready to take cover behind the bar at the first hint of hot lead or discouraging words.

"Coffee, please," she said, clutching her purse on her lap. "And a restroom."

"Restroom's outside. In back." The bartender jerked his thumb toward a door Jenna hadn't noticed before. She nodded, but decided, after a moment's consideration, that she could wait. She was here now, and there was some security in the proximity of the bartender and the light. She didn't want to attract any more attention to herself than she had already.

The coffee came in a disposable cup. Jenna paid for it and requested cream, with some idea that she might be able to cool the coffee, gulp it down like medicine and get out of there as quickly as possible. The bartender gave her a look and brought her a little packet of powder.

Maybe I should have ordered a soda, she thought uneasily as she stirred the coffee with a tiny plastic wand. She'd been noticing that there was virtually nothing in the place that was easily breakable; drinks were served in cans or disposable cups, and there were no bottles or glasses in evidence behind the bar. The significance of that was impossible to ignore.

It was also impossible to ignore the fact that the other patrons' interest in her was beginning to pick up. She'd been hoping it wouldn't. She was, after all, very ordinary looking, with her common brown hair and medium blue eyes and wholesome freckles. She'd known since puberty that she wasn't going to be the sort of woman to make heads turn, and consequently she never had.

That is, she now conceded, unless she was so obviously in the wrong place that she couldn't help but stick out like a sore thumb.

Presently, while Jenna was blowing on her coffee and trying her best to blend into the rustic woodwork, a very large biker ambled over to the bar, slapped down some money and asked for a beer. Instead of taking it back to his table, he popped it open, took a long swallow from it and set it on the bar, all the while giving Jenna a look out of the corners of his eyes. Her heart began to beat faster. After a moment the biker began to slide the beer can toward her end of the bar, sort of ambling casually along beside it as if he just happened to be going in that same direction. Around the corner from where she was sitting, the beer came to a halt and the biker straddled a stool.

Jenna didn't mean to look at him. She tried not to. But, oh, Lord, it was impossible not to.

She'd expected tattoos, but the biker's arms were covered with them. Fantastic tattoos—dragons and tigers and weird mythical creatures and grinning skulls. She couldn't help but stare; she'd never seen anything like it. And from there it just wasn't possible to keep her fascinated gaze from creeping on over bulging biceps toward the rolled-up sleeves of a black T-shirt and across the blue denim vest, across acres and acres of belly and chest. Good grief, she thought, the man was built like the front end of a truck! Beyond that she dared snatch only one quick, horrified glance, but it was enough—after all, hers was an artist's eye. Even in that brief moment it all too graphically recorded the fleshy, stubbled jowls, graying, shoulder-length hair, a rolled bandanna tied around a broad, wind-reddened forehead, small, glittery eyes and a tobacco-stained smile.

It was the smile that sent cold chills down Jenna's spine. Because although she'd never seen one like it before, and certainly never directed at her, she knew exactly what it meant. Admittedly her life would have to be considered somewhat sheltered, but she wasn't stupid.

Meanwhile, a second man had detached himself from the crowd in the corner and come to stand behind The Truck, this one smaller and more fit looking, with thinning black hair and a black moustache that drooped past the corners of his mouth. He didn't immediately claim a stool, but lit a cigarette as he appeared to think it over.

Jenna figured it was high time for retreat, however ignominious. There was such a thing as too much pride. But she was afraid she might have waited too long, because now, in order to reach the front exit, she was going to have to pass by those two bikers at a distance somewhat less than arm's length. When she looked at those arms, brown and gnarled and as big around as tree limbs, her courage failed her.

All things considered, she decided it was probably safer to stay where she was, finish her coffee, ignore the bikers and hope for the best. Maybe they would leave before she did. And even if they did approach her, talk to her or—what was that expression?—put the move on her?—she'd just tell them she wasn't interested. What could they possible do here, in a public bar at four o'clock in the afternoon?

The answer that occurred to her did nothing to ease her mind. She may have lead a sheltered life, but she read the newspapers. These men looked big and tough and mean, and for the first time she realized that she might be in real trouble.

The Truck drank more beer and made rumbling noises that were apparently a prologue to speech. In her panic, Jenna quickly and unwisely gulped hot coffee.

"Hey, take it easy, darlin'," a soft voice drawled in her ear. "Don't burn yourself."

A bolt of adrenaline shot like a silvered arrow through her body. Oh, God, another one, she thought, brushing scalding liquid off the back of her hand with shaking fingers. Now she was as good as surrounded. But where on earth had this one come from? She hadn't noticed anyone sitting behind her, over in the shadowy corners beyond the sound equipment. As the biker eased himself onto the stool next to hers, her heart began a slow, heavy pounding.

"Atta girl, take your time," he murmured approvingly. "Stay awhile."

His voice was something between a purr and a growl. It had a peculiar effect on Jenna. Air seemed to back up in her chest; her skin grew hot.

The biker chuckled knowingly and threw a brief but meaningful look at his two compatriots, a look that held both covenant and challenge. In response to it, The Truck grinned and hunched over his beer; Black Moustache threw his cigarette down on the plank floor and ground it out with his boot, then leaned against the bar, frankly eavesdropping.

"What's your name, pretty lady?" the biker beside her asked in that self-confident, seductive voice. And then, in an altogether different voice, a terse whisper that carried no farther than Jenna's ears: "Talk to me. For Chrissake, flirt with me a little. If they think you're mine, they'll leave you alone."

Startled and confused, light-headed with ebbing adrenaline, Jenna stared at the man, really looking at him for the first time. What she saw made her believe him. Nobody in his right mind would dispute this man's claim, she thought. Nobody would dare.

Once again, though she didn't want to she couldn't help but stare, with the petrified fascination of a rabbit in thrall of the hawk. Part of her—the artist part again—couldn't help but admire the superb muscle definition in those arms and shoulders, the fine, strong facial bones, proud arrogance of nose, cleft chin and wind-blown sweep of dark golden hair. But another part of her, the feminine part, recoiled instinctively in primal fear of such overpowering masculinity—and then returned, reluctantly attracted by a magnetism she could neither understand nor deny.

It was the eyes, she thought. Black as ink, deep and hard and fearless. They issued a challenge no sane man would care to answer, one that no woman could resist.

"Jenna," she heard herself say. "Jenna . . . M-miller."

She never knew what remnant of good sense or self-preservation made her utter that lie. She'd been staring at the sign above the bar advertising a popular brand of beer, and for some reason at the last moment, emphatically if not smoothly, substituted it for her own name.

The biker accepted it with a smile. "Jenna. That's better. You here for the music?"

"Music?"

He motioned with his head toward the cluster of speakers and music stands. "Ernie Rose's band. Pretty good country, a little bluegrass." There were men there now, all wearing plaid shirts and cowboy hats, fussing with the microphones and talking in undertones to each other. Jenna hadn't seen them come in.

She hurriedly shook her head. "I just stopped for coffee. I really don't think—I have to be going."

"You walk out of here now, alone, and you're fair game," the biker said, turning his head to bring his lips close to her ear. "Stay here with me awhile. Relax, drink your coffee, listen to a little country music. When the time's right, I'll see you to your car."

Stay with me awhile. A strange little shiver rippled down Jenna's back. She opened her mouth to demur and encountered the man's eyes, so close to her now she could see they weren't black after all, but dark, dark brown, the pupils fully dilated in the dim light. The words she'd meant to utter ran away from her like water on hot sand.

This is crazy, she thought. If she understood him right, this man—this biker—was offering her protection from the others, a clear case, it seemed to her, of the fire offering to save her from the frying pan. Because of all the rough-hewn, hard-bitten men in that place, *he* looked the most dangerous. Not as big as The Truck, perhaps, nor as wiry-mean as Black Moustache, but she had no doubt whatsoever that in any kind of fight, he could taken them both on and win. Except, she thought, that it wasn't ever likely to come to fighting. A man would have to be crazy to tangle with him. He seemed . . . invincible.

The biker had pivoted on his stool so that he was facing her, with his back against the bar. "Hey, sweet lady," he said, chuckling easily, "don't look at me like that. I'm not the big bad wolf."

Now that he'd turned around, Jenna saw that he had a tattoo on his shoulder—it appeared to be a falcon, or perhaps an eagle. She focused on it and made a small throat-clearing sound. "I was thinking of a fox."

There was a muffled sound—a snicker?—from one of the listening bikers. Jenna's "protector" ignored it. He touched the back of her hand with his forefingers, ignoring, too, her slight, involuntary flinch. "Fox?"

"*The Fox and the Gingerbread Man*," Jenna explained, fighting to keep her voice steady. There was a hot shaft through the middle of her chest. It seemed to have some connection to the finger that was moving slowly back and forth along the tendons of her hand, but try as she would, she couldn't make herself break that contact. It was as if he'd pinned her hand to the bar with just that feather-light touch. "You know the story."

"No," he said in his deep, rumbling purr. "I don't think I do. Tell me."

Feeling a bit silly, Jenna cleared her throat. "The gingerbread man was running away. The fox offered to help him across a river. On the way, he ate him."

This time The Truck was less successful in stifling his guffaw. Black Moustache stirred appreciatively as he lit another cigarette, then settled once more into his casually watchful slouch. The blond biker picked up a book of matches the other man had just tossed on the bar and frowned at it for a moment or two. When his dark gaze came back to Jenna, it was very intent and not in the least affected by his smile.

"Is that what you're doing? Running away?"

Jenna sipped coffee and placed her cup carefully on the counter. "That's not the point of the story," she said, turning her head to look at him.

"Oh, yeah? What is?"

He was mocking her. It wasn't really necessary to an-swer, so she didn't. It took all her poise and courage just to meet those dark, relentless eyes. As she did, the focus in them intensified and narrowed, and before she knew what was happening she was caught, sucked in, held fast. The room, musicians, bartender and the other bikers disap-peared. Silence engulfed her.

There was a chuckle so soft it seemed part of the silence, and then, "Darlin', I'm not planning to eat you."

Jenna muttered, "Funny, that's just what the fox said, too."

The biker snorted, but before he could answer that, the microphone gave a warning whine.

"Evenin', folks," said an amplified voice with a mellow, southwestern twang. "We'd like to start things off right with a little bit of bluegrass. Here's one ya'll know..."

A violin struck some chords that were greeted with anti-cipatory applause and a few cowboy yells from the other end of the room. Guitars and a banjo picked up the tune, and the applause evolved into rhythmic clapping.

Jenna drew a breath of relief and turned to watch, feel-ing obscurely shaken, as if she'd been released from a spell only by some quirk of fortune.

A bikers' hangout, country music—dear God, she thought, what am I doing here? She felt like a visitor from another country—another planet!—trying to grope her way through a dangerous situation with an unfamiliar language and alien customs, always aware that the wrong word, the wrong move might bring disaster.

This crazy conversation with the golden-haired biker—if it could be called conversation—was this really the way people talked to each other in bars, with so much tension, so many undercurrents, so few words, so many hidden meanings? How different it was from the cocktail-party conversation she was used to, intelligent, articulate banter that most of the time meant nothing at all. Jenna didn't

really enjoy such social small talk, but at least she understood it. She felt comfortable with it. Safe. Uninvolved.
Unthreatened.

She'd always moved through the world of gallery openings and artists' shows and formal receptions with poise and
confidence—why not, it was her world. She'd been born to
it, raised in it. As the daughter of two of the most re-
nowned painters of the twentieth century, her own success
had come easily, almost as a birthright. Her brief and
memorable sojourn in Paris had been generously spon-
sored. She'd never experienced the misery and glory of life
as a starving artist, which she rather imagined was over-
rated in any case, and had certainly never felt deprived in
missing. Even her college years, which she'd endured for her
parents' sake and which she considered of value only for the
sake of Nancy's friendship, had passed largely unnoticed.
Painting was, and had always been, her world and her life.

*And Jack Remington was an inextricable part of that
world, that life. How could she hope to excise that part of
herself and remain whole?*

She pushed the thought aside and fought off the wave of
panic that always came with it. She had to deal with the here
and now, and she wasn't at all sure how to go about it.
Nothing in her experience had prepared her for men like
these. In the insular world of an artist prodigy, men wore
suits and ties, or at the very least, turtlenecks and tweed.
They smelled of cologne and the unmistakable aura of
money, and followed the social rules. Conversations with
such men were easy, as stylized as a minuet. But this was
different. Jenna didn't know how to talk to men who wore
shirts with no sleeves and jeans that looked as though they'd
been slept in. She didn't know what to expect of them. If she
wanted to leave, would they really try to stop her? How far
would they go?

She stole a look at the two bikers on her left. The Truck
lifted his beer and leered at her, while Black Moustache gave
her a look through a cloud of cigarette smoke, a narrow,

measuring stare. Jenna smiled weakly and went back to watching the band. Those two, at least, appeared capable of anything.

"Looks to me like it's all up to you," the golden-haired biker said, his voice raised just enough for her to hear over the music. He was leaning back with his arms spread wide on the bar, relaxed, confident, idly turning the matches over and over in his fingers. He waved them at her, his gaze dark and quiet. "You know, you're going to have to decide pretty soon whether or not to trust me."

Jenna swallowed and closed her eyes. If this was a dance, she didn't know the steps.

"You like bluegrass?" The biker abruptly shifted gears, making his tone conversational.

Blue grass? Oh, yes, the music. Jenna opened her eyes and blinked the band into focus.

"If you relax, open up a little," the biker went on, "it gets into your bones. You know, you just can't help but feel good, listening to bluegrass."

It was an unexpected thing for such a man to say. Jenna threw him a quick, startled glance, but he was looking at the band, not her. His profile was serene; she noticed a fan of crow's feet at the corner of his eye. Confused and oddly stirred, she forced her attention back to the music.

There were four musicians, a bass guitarist backing up the solo virtuosity of banjo, guitar and violin. Their style was low-key but intent; they played without flash, in the easy manner of friends jamming in someone's living room, concentrating on the music, letting it have the limelight. As each one took his solo turn and then passed it on with a nod and a smile, the small but enthusiastic crowd shouted approval. Jenna just watched in awed silence, mesmerized by the intricate motions of the fingers, the lightning-quick strokes of the bow.

Then the bass player leaned into the microphone and in a curiously high, nasal voice began to sing of lost loves and piney woods, of mountaintops in Tennessee. When he had finished, the violin picked up the melody again, singing of the same things without words. Jenna found that her body wanted to move with the beat, so she let it.

"They're very good," she said breathlessly when the music ended, joining in the applause. "Especially the one on the violin."

The biker chuckled. "*Fiddle*, darlin'. You call it a fiddle."

"Oh," Jenna said. "Of course. I knew that."

The fiddler struck new chords and the music began again, not bluegrass this time, but a slower song, with an unmistakable country sound. The banjo player took the microphone and began to sing about faithless lovers and broken hearts and how much it hurt to say goodbye. And somehow, before she knew what was happening, Jenna had a lump in her throat and tears in her eyes. *Oh, God, yes, it hurts....*

She felt a touch on her shoulder. A rough-soft voice said, "Come on, dance with me."

Jenna glanced at the golden-haired biker, startled for a moment or two to see him there. Startled, too, by the searching look in his eyes. She turned quickly away, blinking.

Dance? To her surprise, she saw now that on the bare wood floor in front of the band, several couples were, indeed, dancing, bikers and their ladies, dressed much the same in blue denim and black leather and Western-style boots. Jenna let a deep breath fill her, easing both her fears and the pain in her heart, fanning new sparks of anger and recklessness. She looked back at the biker. "Dance ... with you?"

"Yeah." He unfolded himself from the bar stool and stood up, holding out his hand. "It's called the Texas two-step. Basic country stuff. Come on, I'll show you how."

He was smiling, but it wasn't the smile that captured her. It was his eyes, black and compelling as a wizard's enchantment. She felt a pulse beating deep in her belly, felt a shiver ripple through her—excitement or nervousness—which one she didn't know or care. She put her hand in his and felt the warmth of it course through her body.

"What do I call you?" she asked, her voice breathless.

His hand tightened on hers; she saw the muscles twist beneath the smooth skin of his forearm. His laughter gusted warm on her forehead as he pulled her toward him.

"Just call me Reno," he said.

Two

It was a name he'd borrowed on the spur of the moment from the book of matches he'd been fiddling with, advertising a casino in Reno, Nevada. It wasn't that he really thought she'd recognize him, although there were still a lot of people who remembered Nathan Wells. It was just that he'd been protecting his privacy for a long time. It had gotten to be a habit with him.

"Reno?" she asked with doubt in her voice and a catch in her breathing.

He didn't answer, just smiled and turned her toward him. Her hand hovered, then came to rest on his shoulder, a shy, tentative weight, like a bird lighting on a swaying reed. He could feel the nervousness in it, soaking through the fabric of his shirt like perspiration.

"Here, darlin', not like that," he said as he positioned his own hand not on her back, but on her shoulder. With his other hand he took hers and guided it into place on the front of his arm. "It goes right here, like this."

She murmured, "Well, that's...different."

He could see her throat move as she swallowed, feel her fingers stirring on his skin, their touch exploratory, inquisitive. Her lashes were lowered, her lips not quite closed. He could see a faint sheen on her eyelids and across the tops of her cheeks.

"Yeah, that's country style," he drawled, his smile sardonic. "See there, I'm giving you plenty of room—so you don't think I'm planning to eat you."

Her eyes snapped to his face, a dead giveaway. So she was still thinking about that fox. Lord, he thought, *The Fox and the Gingerbread Man*. A fairy tale—helluva metaphor. But it had jolted him, because he'd thought of one almost like it when she first walked into the place. A wounded doe, he'd said to himself then. Just one step ahead of the wolves.

He didn't know how to let her know that he wasn't the wolf—or the fox, either.

"Ready?" he murmured. "Just a basic two-step...here we go now."

She missed a beat and made a small, embarrassed sound.

He growled, "You're doin' fine, darlin', just relax a little bit." When she caught her lower lip between her teeth, he was sorry for the roughness in his voice.

Damn it, he wished he could talk to her better, the light and meaningless, smooth and flirty kind of conversation she was probably used to. That would put her at ease. He'd been good at it, once—glib and full of himself, cocky as a rooster on the henhouse roof. How he'd eaten it up, in those days, all that recognition, not to mention adoration, from the groupies and the dugout dolls...

But that had been a while ago and he'd forgotten the lingo. Besides, this was different. This was a lady, not a doll. And it was harder when he was the one wanting to know all about *her*, instead of the other way around.

She'd shifted her eyes downward again, so she was staring right at his chin. He figured she was doing that because he made her nervous, but he didn't mind because this way he could look at her all he wanted to without her knowing. Looking at her, he'd discovered, was something he enjoyed doing. Not that he hadn't seen prettier women and dated more than a few, too, but there was something about this woman he liked, something fresh and inherently classy. She felt light in his arms and smelled good—not sweet and perfumed, but of something that reminded him of sunshine and breezes blowing through new grass. Her hair, right about on a level with his mouth, was thick and glossy and so clean it moved with a life of its own, making him wonder what it would be like to bury his face and hands in it.

"I think I'm getting it," she said, a little out of breath. And then the song ended.

She jerked her hand off of his arm as if she'd been caught in a shameful act and threw a quick, nervous look over her shoulder. Sure enough, the two bikers were still sitting at the bar, leering back at her.

"Stay here," Nate commanded softly, aware of the shudder that ran through her. "They'll start another one in a minute—right Ernie?" He leaned over and tapped the fiddler's music stand with his knuckle.

The boys were playing random chords and muttering among themselves about what they were going to play next. Ernie Rose looked over at Nate and grinned. A mellow chuckle came through the microphone. "Well now, this here's where we usually do some patter—you know, where we say how glad we are to be here and tell you a little bit about our next song, but...looks to me like all ya'll want to do is dance. And I gotta say, if I had a sweet, pretty little thing like that in my arms, I'd wanna do that, too. So here's a dancin' tune...." He put his fiddle under his chin and struck the chords.

"Oh," Jenna said with a pleased smile, "a waltz. This one I know how to do." She stepped up with confidence and put her hand on Nate's arm. But when her fingers touched his skin, something happened to her confidence; he could feel her flinch, feel the slight break in her breathing. Her mouth opened and her eyes flew up to his face. There was a puzzled look in them, as if she'd started to say something and then forgotten what it was.

Nate hesitated a moment, then slipped his arm around her waist. Still watching him, still puzzled, she slid her hand up to the back of his neck. "That's right," he murmured, and drew her closer. Not against him, just...closer. Holding her like that, he couldn't look at her anymore. All he could do was feel her and think about her.

He felt her sweater, soft against his palm, and under it her her back, firm and supple and warm. He thought about the tiny little space between his body and hers, about how much he wanted to close it and how easy it would be to do so if he chose to force the issue. He felt the moist puff of her breath cool the sweat at the base of his neck, and he thought about her eyes and the lost look he'd seen in them. He wondered who or what she was running away from and who might have hurt her.

Influenced by the direction his thoughts were taking, his hand moved on her back, a natural kind of stroking. Her gaze bounced right up to his face, a wary light in them that may have been a question or a warning.

"Relax," he muttered as much to himself as to her. And then, because the song was one he knew and liked, he began to hum it, a risky undertaking, considering how bad a singer he was. It did have the desired effect, though. She smiled and began to move easier, evidently figuring a man who was humming a waltz off-key in her ear couldn't have too much wickedness on his mind.

This time when the song ended, she didn't seem so quick to jump out of his arms. She waited with him, self-conscious but eager, while Ernie introduced his band and then the next song, a slow one, an old Patsy Cline tearjerker. Ernie did the singing himself on this one, in that tenor voice of his that could make a stone cry. And this time, when Jenna came into Nate's arms, he didn't have to show her how. She put her hand on the back of his neck and he put his arm around her, and she came to him as naturally as breathing.

"Atta girl," he said approvingly.

She said something he didn't hear, so he lowered his head and asked her to repeat it. She murmured, "'Jump up on my nose, said the fox.'"

Damn that fox. Nate pulled back just far enough to see her face—and to his surprise found that she was smiling and that there was a look in her eyes that he hadn't seen there before, a cool blue spark of daring. That spark ignited something in him, something he hadn't felt in a long time. Damned if it wasn't . . . *excitement*. It flared in his belly and blew through him like a chinook, bringing warmth and wreaking havoc on his senses. Even the air felt different to him. Chuckling softly, he eased her back against him.

Lost lady, who are you? Where have you come from and where are you going?

He felt bemused, intrigued as he hadn't been in a long time, wondering about the woman dancing in his arms. He wanted to know everything about her. Her name—her real name, not the one she'd given him, which he was pretty sure was about as genuine as the one he'd given her. He hadn't questioned that or even asked himself why she'd done it; maintaining anonymity with strangers was natural behavior to him. But right now he was thinking he'd like to get her to trust him enough so she'd tell him her real one. And even thinking that maybe, just maybe, someday he'd tell her his.

He replied to her comment about the fox with an ambiguous grunt, and shifted his arm a little, subtly impelling her still closer. He felt no resistance in her. In fact as her body came against his, he felt her relax, as if something she'd been dreading for a long time had failed to come about. Her fingers moved on the back of his neck, toying in a shy and cautious way with the ends of his hair. He turned his head slightly, testing the softness of hers with his chin.

She felt good. Too good. This time when the song ended, it was he who separated himself from her, establishing a barrier of safe space between their bodies. A barrier that somehow melted away like a heat mirage when the music began again.

It felt good, her warmth seeping through his shirt and into his skin, the play of muscle beneath his hand, the slip and slide of her thighs over his. Boldly, though unconsciously at first, he began to use his body to say to her the things he couldn't say with words, swaying and bending with the music in ways that came easily to him after all the years of physical conditioning. It was a sensual seduction, but one so subtle she didn't seem to be aware of what was happening. In fact, neither was he until he heard her quickening breath, felt her heart pounding against his chest and realized that his own body rhythms were timing themselves to hers. He made himself stop it, not because it wasn't what he wanted, but because his body's obvious response to her wasn't going to help reassure her he wasn't that damn fox after all.

"Water's risin'," he muttered under his breath, but when she murmured a drowsy, "Hmm?" he cleared his throat, nodded toward the bar and said instead, "Looks like the Hardy Boys have gone home."

"Oh, yes." She glanced at the two vacant bar stools that until recently had been occupied by bikers—friends of Nate's and mostly harmless, though she didn't have to know that. "So I see."

But her eyes seemed unfocused and she came back into Nate's arms like a wanderer returning to where she belonged.

They sat down a couple of times during the bluegrass numbers, which were more for listening than dancing. During those times Nate discovered that he liked watching the lady almost as much as he liked dancing with her. Watching her move with the beat, her face alight with excitement, made him feel as if he were seeing and hearing it all over again for the first time. As if he'd never before seen fingers move across a banjo's strings like sunlight on wind-riffled water, never heard a fiddler coax laughter and tears from his instrument with nothing but a wooden stick strung with horsehair. He remembered that he'd once thought there was magic in music, because he was no good at it himself. Now for the first time in years, watching the awe in her face, he felt the magic again.

The last song the band played was another waltz, one he'd heard before, a song about cheating lovers, so sad and lonely it made you want to hold on tight to the woman in your arms and never let go. On about the third chorus the woman in Nate's arms began to sing along softly, in a voice as clear and sweet as a spring morning. And for some reason it got to him. He almost had to laugh at himself, the way a tough, macho man laughs, kind of embarrassed, when he's caught misting up in a sad movie.

The music ended and Ernie's mellow, Southern voice came in on the dying chords. "That's it, folks. We'd like to thank ya'll for listenin'. Hope to see ever'body next Thursday night, right back here at the Old Coach Station. G'night, now..."

The lady, Jenna Miller or whatever her real name was, stirred and pulled back a little, looking dazed and disoriented, as if she'd just woken up from a nap. Nate let his arms drop away from her.

"Looks like that's it," he said, clearing his throat with a husky cough. "They're packin' it in."

She stared at her watch, then around her at the almost empty place. "Oh, God," she muttered, "I can't believe— I've got to go!"

Maybe it was that nursery-tale metaphor she'd been using on him all night, but the way she threw him a wild look, grabbed up her purse and headed for the door, she made Nate think of Cinderella hearing the first knell of the clock.

Beyond the door they could hear the muted thunder of a dozen or so Harleys coming to life. Nate just did manage to get to the door before she did, muttering, "Well, hold on a minute, damn it." He felt like the prince hollering, "Wait, don't go!" as the girl of his dreams sprinted for the palace stairs.

When his hand met hers on the doorknob, she hesitated, looking up at him. He heard the unevenness of her breathing and saw, even in that dim light, the shine of something in her eyes, something he couldn't put a name to, that once again excited him in a way he'd all but forgotten.

He growled, "I want to see you again," then thought, Ah shoot, too blunt. Too forceful. But he didn't have time for finesse, especially since it didn't come naturally to him.

She didn't answer. He didn't really expect her to. Looking confused and dismayed, she shook her head and pushed open the door.

Outside, the night had taken on the noisy surrealism of a rock video, with the beat of all those big bikes revving up, dust swirling yellow-gold in the headlights, taillights fading into the distance like dying coals, voices calling to each other across the chaos. Several of them called out to Nate, too, and called him by name, but he didn't think Jenna even noticed.

He stood patiently with one hand on the roof of her car while she fumbled in her purse for her keys. When she came up with them, he took them and opened the door for her, then held it while she got in and buckled her seat belt.

"You gonna tell me how I can get in touch with you?" he asked her as he handed back the keys.

Again her mouth dropped open, as if there was something she wanted to say but didn't quite have the nerve. As she was taking the keys from him, her fingers touched his and she jerked away from the contact, as if she'd touched a hot wire. "I'm sorry," she gasped as she stabbed the key blindly at the ignition. "I don't—I'm sorry, I can't. Someone's expecting me. I have to go." There was panic in her voice.

Nate stepped away from the car and held out his hands. "Darlin'," he said gently, "I'm not stopping you."

For a long three count she sat there with her hand on the gearshift, then kind of relaxed back in her seat and looked up at him, just looked, with her eyes reflecting little pinpoints of colored light from the Station's windows. It hit him then—desire, like a hunger in his belly, a gnawing, twisting hunger that grew more insistent the longer she looked at him.

The last of the big bikes growled away into the night and in the quiet left behind, Nate spoke softly. "Hey, you know, I'm not the big bad wolf or that fox or whatever in the hell it is you're afraid of."

She considered that for a moment, then tilted her head and asked just as softly, "What are you, then?"

Off in the creek bed, some frogs started filling the night with their own music. Somewhere a door slammed. Nate said, "What do you want me to be?"

There was a faint sound, a little stumble in the rapid pace of her breathing. Her lips parted, and as that spark of daring flared in her eyes, the hunger in Nate's belly became a bonfire. But she didn't say anything, so after a few moments he gave her a lopsided smile and a wave, then turned and walked away. It wasn't easy, but as much as he didn't want this woman driving out of his life, he knew there wasn't anything to be gained by pushing her. And he'd learned a long time ago that you never, ever let an opponent—or a woman—know when they've got you on the ropes.

"So long, darlin'," he said as he straddled his bike. "You take care, now."

All the while he was shrugging into his jacket and lifting his helmet off the handlebars, he knew that she was still sitting there with the motor running, the car door hanging open and an expression on her face that reminded him of the way she'd looked watching the banjo picker, rapt and shining.

"A black night," she said suddenly.

"Yeah, it is," Nate agreed, looking up into it and then glancing over at her, wondering why on earth she'd mentioned it now.

She shook her head. "No, I mean, that's what you look like. A *knight*." Smiling, she nodded toward the helmet he was holding in his hands, its visor reflecting her car's headlights like polished steel. "With your helmet and charger."

"Charger?" Nate looked down at the powerful machine between his thighs, then threw back his head and laughed out loud. The lady sure had one helluva strange imagination. He gunned the bike's engine a couple of times, then balanced the helmet on the gas tank and kicked off. Maybe showing off a little bit, too, he acknowledged as he eased up alongside her car, letting the bike idle at high rev—like a warhorse champing at the bit?—while he leaned over to speak to her.

"Okay, I'll be your knight, if that's what you want. And what does that make you," he asked, still laughing, raising his voice above the throbbing engine, "a lady in distress?"

He saw, rather than heard, her quick intake of breath, her nervous, shaken laughter, and knew he'd hit pretty near the truth. But he only said, "So long, darlin'," and smiled at her as he pulled on his helmet.

As he dug out with a modest spatter of gravel, he wasn't surprised to hear her call, "Reno, wait!"

He paused to look back. She'd shut the door and rolled down the window and was leaning out of it with one hand cupped around her mouth. "I'm staying with a friend," she shouted. "Her number's 555-6279."

Nate lifted one hand to his helmet in a salute that held more mockery than acknowledgment. Because he knew she still didn't trust him, and that common sense and all the things she'd ever been taught about talking to strangers were still doing battle with the dynamite attraction between them, as well as with a latent sense of adventure he'd bet she didn't even know she had. Because, damn her, he knew good and well she was figuring he'd forget that phone number before he got to a place where he could write it down.

Nevertheless, he was laughing as he spun out onto the paved road and accelerated into the quiet night, feeling exhilarated and young and springtime wild. What the lady didn't know, was that memorizing numbers was second nature to a ballplayer, especially a pitcher, who had to be able to call up the statistics on every batter he faced. It had been a while, but he hadn't lost the knack.

And even if he forgot the telephone number, which he wasn't about to do, he'd already mentally copied down the license number of her car.

Lady, he thought, fox, wolf or renegade knight, you're going to be seeing me again. You can count on it.

"Jen, is that you? Oh, thank God, you're finally here." Nancy came skipping down the steps to the driveway, holding out her arms, alternately laughing and scolding. "I'm so glad you're all right. When you called, I was about five seconds away from calling the highway patrol, I want you to know that. You really had me *worried*."

The last word was emphasized by an enormous bear hug that left Jenna gasping for air. Nancy was small but strong, and her enthusiasm could be exhausting. As her roommate in college, Jenna had been known to seek the relative peace and quiet of the student union when there was serious studying to be done. She still found it hard to understand how the dearest and noisiest of all her friends had managed to become, of all things, a small-town librarian.

"*God*, it's good to see you! Gee, Jen, you look great. In fact—" Nancy pulled back, squinting suspiciously. "You really do look great. How come? Aren't you supposed to be all pale and wan? What happened to that poor heartbroken creature I invited for a week of succor, solace and serious girl talk? Your eyes are positively sparkling. Last time I talked to you, you sounded like you had a bad case of hay fever. Does this mean you're over Jack Remington once and for all, I hope, I hope?''

Jenna, who in the midst of all this had unlocked the trunk of her car and begun the process of unloading it, used that activity to cover the automatic convulsion in her throat and rush of prickles to her eyes. "No," she said, "I'm not over Jack."

She didn't add that she wasn't ever going to get over Jack, which was a sure way to send Nancy off on a tirade. Instead, hoping to head her off, Jenna plunked a suitcase at her friend's feet and puffed, "I just did something totally insane. I can't believe I did it. You aren't going to believe it, either."

"Oh, good," Nancy said avidly. "Tell me."

"Well, I just had a fling," Jenna said. "With a biker."

"Uh-huh." There was a pause. Nancy said, "I take it you do not mean the kind with those short, shiny, skintight pants?"

Jenna slowly shook her head and gulped down a bubble of laughter. "Nope. But he had a tattoo."

"Oh, Jenna, my dear child," Nancy said gravely as she picked up the suitcase.

The nice thing about Nancy, and one of the reasons Jenna had so readily accepted her invitation—one of the reasons, in fact, why they'd remained friends for so long—was that she was as enthusiastic a listener as everything else. Once the suitcases had been summarily deposited in the spare bedroom, she made tea—something without caffeine that smelled wonderfully of apples and cinnamon and tasted of nothing much in particular. Then she waved Jenna to a stool, levered herself onto the counter and ordered, "Okay, m'dear, let's have it. You just had a fling with a biker, you said. Not that I can speak from experience, of course, but I don't think one *flings* with bikers, if you know what I mean. So tell me what happened."

Jenna wrapped her hands around the mug of tea and inhaled the spicy aroma, stalling for time. She needed a moment because her emotions, always close to the surface these days, were threatening to spring forth again. And though she'd never cared much for herbal tea, there was something about the warmth of it that seemed to find its way clear down to her battered heart.

"It was funny," she said finally with a little gust of shaken laughter. "I just stopped for a cup of coffee, you know? At this little out-of-the-way place. And it turned out to be some sort of bikers' hangout. I know I shouldn't have gone in by myself. I don't know why I did—you know me, I wouldn't ordinarily—but for some reason I just felt as if nothing mattered anyway, so..." She stopped, blinking rapidly.

"We are going to have to do something about this," Nancy muttered darkly, "but we'll get to that later. Ahem, please continue."

She listened attentively until Jenna got to the part about the third biker sitting down beside her. She was trying to describe his voice and the strange effect it had had on her, when Nancy suddenly interrupted to ask, "What did this guy look like?"

What had he looked like? Ah, but that was the easy part. She closed her eyes and was back there again, in the bikers' bar, with the atmosphere redolent of cigarette smoke and beer and old, old wood....

"Tall," she said on a long, indrawn breath, "but not too tall." No, not too tall; she had come just about to his nose...she'd felt the warmth of his breath in her hair. "Umm...big, but not heavy. Well-built. He seemed...fit." *Fit?* What an insipid way to describe those beautiful, sculpted muscles...the feel of that strong, sinewy body moving against hers....

"Jen," Nancy said, "you're blushing."

Jenna coughed and opened her eyes. "Um, let's see...he had a tattoo. Right here." She tapped her own shoulder. *His* shoulder had been so firm, so vibrant, so warm...his skin nut-brown and smooth, like satin beneath her fingertips.

"You mentioned the tattoo," Nancy impatiently reminded her. "What about his hair? Light or dark? Did he have a beard?"

"No beard. In fact..." She paused, smiling a little. In fact, he'd had a very nice chin. With a definite cleft in it. "Wait, give me something—" She made impatient motions with her hands, which Nancy, being accustomed to them, correctly interpreted. She quickly produced a notepad and pencil that she slapped down on the counter in front of Jenna. Jenna snatched up the pencil and began to draw with quick, bold strokes.

"His hair—dark blond, I think..." She spoke the way she drew, in bursts of breathless, disconnected phrases. "Streaks of gold, all wavy and windblown...like this." And he had smelled of the wind, too, and sunshine and rich brown earth.... "The most incredible eyes. So dark...so intense." So dark you could see yourself reflected in them, along with all the desires you'd ever dared dream and never dared reveal to anyone. A sorcerer's eyes.

"So-o," Nancy prompted, trying to get a look at the drawing, "you talked with this biker?"

"Well, actually," Jenna said absently, "he didn't say very much."

"Uh-huh. Okay then, what did you do?"

"We danced...."

Nancy put her hand over her eyes and whispered, "Oh my stars."

"It sort of just happened," Jenna explained, looking up. "There was a band. Country music and bluegrass. I guess I must have heard bluegrass music before—I know I'd heard *of* it—but I'd never actually heard it performed live. Nancy, it's incredible." She smiled, remembering. Her hands lay motionless on the notepad. "Reno said it gets into your bones, and you can't help but feel good."

"*Reno?* Oh my God."

"Yes, that's his name. Reno."

"Yeah," Nancy said dryly. "Right."

"Well, all right, so maybe that's not his real name," Jenna said, giggling. "But I didn't give him my real name, either."

"Thank God!"

Jenna smothered her laughter with her hand and muttered through it, "I gave him your phone number."

"You *what*?"

"Oh, don't worry, he won't remember it—I just shouted it at him as he was riding off on his motorcycle. I don't know what got into me. I really don't. I was—" She stopped and stared down at the face on the notepad. After a moment she turned it around and slid it slowly along the tile countertop.

Nancy picked it up, looked at it for a second or two and then uttered a reverent, "Oh my." After a silence of unprecedented duration, she tore her eyes away from the drawing and prompted gently, "And you were...?"

"Confused," Jenna whispered.

"Confused?" Nancy frowned, then with the rare understanding and the bluntness that made her such a dear and valued friend said, "You mean because of Jack. Because you felt things for this...this Reno, and you don't think you should."

Miserably, Jenna nodded. "Nancy, I loved Jack as deeply as it's possible to love someone. You know that. It wasn't a crush, or—or some sort of infatuation, it was *real*."

Jenna got up and paced a few steps, hugging herself and hugging to herself the pain that had become her almost constant companion. Jack Remington had been such an important part of her life for so many years. The Remington Gallery had been her second—and perhaps her real—home. Separating herself from both of them at the same time had been... "I didn't know it was possible to hurt like that," she said in a whisper. "I thought I was hurting before the break and that ending the relationship was the way to end the pain, but—"

"It was, believe me," Nancy stated fervently. "Just give yourself time."

"Then why do I feel so much worse? It's been weeks, and it's not getting any better! At least—until . . ."

"Until tonight."

Jenna turned slowly. "Yes. Almost from the first moment I walked into that place, I felt . . . I don't know, this kind of excitement. And once I got over being afraid, when we started to dance and I touched him—just on the arm, like this—I felt . . . Nancy, I felt *attracted* to him."

Nancy burst out laughing. "For goodness sake, Jen, don't sound so shocked. Of course you were attracted to him! Look at this guy. My God, he's dynamic!"

Ignoring that, not joining in the laughter, Jenna said, "And it suddenly occurred to me that I hadn't thought of Jack all evening. And that I didn't hurt. And the terrible part of it is, that I feel guilty—more than guilty. I felt as if something was missing. Nancy, I felt . . . kind of a sense of *loss*. Because the pain was gone. Does that make any sense at all?"

"Of course it does," Nancy said comfortably, getting up to refill the tea cups. "The pain is all you have left of Jack. When it's gone—and it will go, believe me—you'll be free of him. You're still holding on, that's all. You just have to let go—I mean really let go. You can do it—you did it when your mom and dad died. Let yourself heal, darlin'."

Darlin'. . . With the unexpected reprise of a soft-rough voice rippling through her, Jenna drew an unsteady breath and said, "But, Nan, I still love Jack. Facing up to the fact that it was never going to work out between us didn't change that. And to be so attracted to a another man—I just don't see how I can be. What does that make me?"

"Resilient," Nancy said, beaming at her. "Normal. Human." When Jenna just looked at her in mute distress, she shook her head and went on complacently, "It's what I've been telling you all along, Jen. Contrary to what you believe right now, Jack is not the only man in this world for you. You get more than one shot at the brass ring—that's what's so great about life. It's a whole series of new beginnings and fresh starts and second chances. You just have to be open to the possibilities.''

"That's funny," Jenna said with a painful little chuckle, "that's just what I said to Jack, way back at the beginning of all this, when he was going through his divorce." She smiled wryly, rubbing at the familiar ache in her throat. "I suppose," she said thoughtfully after a moment, "Jack must have been hurting as badly then as I am now. He was so open, so vulnerable. All the walls were down. I just couldn't help but fall in love with him, especially since I'd been half in love with him since I was fifteen-years-old anyway."

It had been so wonderful at first. Like a miracle to her. She'd never felt closer to anyone, or felt she knew anyone so well. The man she'd been so in awe of for most of her adult life was suddenly human and reachable. They'd spent hours together, talking, walking, laughing together. She'd come to know his flaws, his shortcomings, his vulnerabilities, and loved him the more for all of them.

"But then..." She drew a deep, shuddering breath. "I guess his wounds started to heal. I mean, I wanted him to heal...." But the walls had gone back up and she had been left outside. "Well, anyway," she said, clearing her throat and trying to keep her tone matter-of-fact, "things got very strange between us. He'd alternate between seeming to want my friendship and pushing me away. Nancy, he wouldn't even allow himself to touch me—not even to take my hand. It was almost as if he—I know this sounds crazy—as if he was afraid of me."

Nancy frowned as she drank hot tea. "Oh, yes, it makes all kinds of sense," she said with a shrug. "You were his heart mender."

"His what?"

"Heart mender. I have single friends who tell me they never, *ever* date a man who's been divorced less than a year because the first relationship after a breakup never sticks. They just wind up patching up some heartbroken guy, only to get dumped when he's got his act together. Well, think about it—it's like when you're really sick and you have to let someone—strangers even—take care of you, bathe you, help you to the bathroom and so forth. And then you get well. As soon as you start feeling better, you want your privacy back, right? And you even feel a little embarrassed around the person who took care of you and who now knows all the horrid, intimate details about you. I think a man—especially a man as proud and private as Jack Remington—would feel at a disadvantage with a woman who knew his human frailties too well. He strikes me as a man who would always have to be in control, give the illusion, at least, of invincibility.''

Jenna sat gazing miserably into her tea. "So," she said dully, "you think that's all I was? Jack's...heart mender?"

"Hey, don't say it like that. Mending hearts is important work. Somebody has to do it or else the world would be littered with nonfunctioning, emotional cripples."

"But damn it," Jenna shouted, sobbing, "it wasn't that for *me*!"

"I know," Nancy said, instantly contrite and compassionate. "I'm sorry, I didn't mean to sound flippant." She put her cup and Jenna's in the sink and came to put her arms around her friend.

"It's just that I hate seeing my best friend in such pain. Hey—Jen, we'll just have to find you your own heart mender! Goodness knows," she said passionately, "I wouldn't even mind if you had a fling with the biker, if it made you feel better."

"Forget it," Jenna said stuffily into a paper napkin, "I'm never going to see *him* again."

"Good, you're laughing. Let's go to bed. We've got days of talking ahead of us. Not to mention some serious shopping. Must keep up our strength." She hooked her arm through Jenna's and dragged her off the stool. Laughing and emotionally exhausted, Jenna went meekly.

On the way up the stairs, Nancy said thoughtfully, "You're right, forget this Reno guy. We can do a lot better than a biker—even one who looks like Hercules with a dimple."

"Not Hercules," Jenna said giggling. "I told him he looked like a knight."

"You didn't!"

"Oh yes, I did." Still giggling, she dropped her voice to a dark and dramatic whisper. "The mysterious Black Knight..."

But, she thought to herself as she went soberly and alone into her room, he has a wizard's eyes.

Merlin's eyes.

Three

———

Jenna woke to the ruckus of mockingbirds in the hibiscus bushes below her window. The noise brought an instant flood of childhood memories, of weekends spent at her grandparents' house in Redding and the mockingbirds who had so loved to torment the yellow tomcat, Jinks, by dive-bombing him from the vantage point of the palm trees in the backyard. Memories of heat, the smell of honeysuckle and old roses. Memories of making hollyhock ladies and playing naked in the sprinkler. Once she'd made a picture of Jinks with her crayons—one of the very first original Jenna McBrides—and Gram had exclaimed over it and taped it to the pantry door. Those summers had been the "normal" times, she realized now, tranquil, sun-dappled eddies in the swift-moving stream of her life.

She stretched extravagantly, enjoying the guilt-free luxury of languishing in bed, then for some reason found herself thinking of the summer of the chicken pox. She must have been ten or eleven, heartbroken not to be allowed to accompany her parents on the usual summer tour of gallery openings. Trying to make her feel better, Grampa had given her a book about King Arthur. It was a very old book, and the language was strange and difficult to understand, but Jenna hadn't minded because it was full of wonderful pictures, beautiful engravings of knights and ladies and unicorns. She had spent that summer happily scratching away at her chicken pox and filling her sketchbooks with colored pencil drawings of Camelot....

Smiling and misty with nostalgia, Jenna rose and padded barefoot to the window to see what was causing the mockingbirds' alarm. Sure enough, a large gray cat was crouched there on the cement-block wall that separated Nancy's house from the neighbor's, pretending, with classic feline disdain, to ignore the angry birds fluttering and screeching around his head. That, however, was where any similarity to those sundrenched memories of childhood ended; the bay was, as usual, fogbound. Jenna smiled sympathetically at the beleaguered cat, trying to hold on to her waking mood, but she could already feel the cold and gloom outside creeping into her heart, stealing the colors from her soul.

Panic clutched at her as it always did when she thought about her art . . . her life, her future. She wondered what Nancy would say if she knew Jenna had stopped painting. But there was nothing left in her to paint *with*—no joy, no passion, no fire—nothing. She was burned out. The child prodigy, finished at thirty.

She had drawn a somewhat unsteady breath and was turning from the window when Nancy knocked and almost simultaneously stuck her head in the door.

"Jenna? Oh, good, you're up," she said briskly, and added, with a carefully deadpan expression, "Telephone for you."

"Good heavens, so early?" Jenna reached for her bathrobe, yawning. "Who is it?"

"It's nearly noon," Nancy mildly informed her. "And . . . he didn't say."

He? And there was something odd about Nancy's tone of voice—suppressed excitement with just a dash of disapproval. A cold wave of mixed hope and dread washed over Jenna, weakening her knees. She put her hand on the bed to steady herself while she pushed her feet into her slippers and murmured, "Not..."

"No," Nancy said stiffly, "not Jack. No one I recognize, but—" she tilted her head thoughtfully "—his voice did strange things to my insides."

Jenna had recently met someone with a voice like that. But it couldn't be—he couldn't have remembered.... She covered her mouth with her hand and gulped. "Oh, God, you don't think it's *him*, do you? That biker?"

"I don't know," Nancy said on the way out the door, "but if you'd quit dithering, we could both find out. Hurry up—I made you some coffee, I know you aren't crazy about herbal tea. Do you still eat graham crackers and milk for breakfast?"

Jenna followed the breathless phrases down the stairs and into the kitchen, where she picked up the telephone and with morning's huskiness still clinging to her voice said, "Hello?"

"Well, Gingerbread Lady. Good mornin'."

The rough-soft voice stroked her auditory nerves like woolen mittens. She sank onto a stool. *"Reno?"*

"Yeah." There was a chuckle, a sound as warming as coffee in the morning. "You sound surprised."

"Well," Jenna admitted, clearing her throat, "I guess I am. I didn't think—"

"You didn't think I'd remember the number. I know." The voice sounded wry. "Hey, I told you I wanted to see you again. You bet I remembered it."

Jenna didn't know what to reply to that, so she didn't.

"Well, say something," the voice on the telephone implored with another of those soft chuckles.

"I'm sorry," she replied truthfully, "I don't know what to say."

There was another pause, and then the sigh of released breath. "Hey, listen, I know right now you're wondering how you could have done such a dumb thing as to give your phone number to some stranger you met in a bar, right? Last night you kind of got caught up in things, maybe you were feelin' a little reckless. But things look and feel different in the cold gray light, and this morning you're afraid you might have gotten yourself in a mess of trouble. Am I hittin' anywhere near the mark?''

"Well," Jenna hedged, and then stopped. "Not at all," she said, trying to sound cool and confident, like a reasonable facsimile of a mature adult. "It's just that I've never met a biker before. I'm not sure what you expect of me. I don't think we'd have very much in common."

This time the pause on the other end of the telephone was long and thoughtful, as if, perhaps, her forthrightness had caught him off guard. Then, very quietly, in the voice that did "things" to a woman's insides, he said, "Darlin', I ride a motorcycle. That's something I do, it's not who I am. I earn my living, I don't do drugs and I'm not into violence, and under extreme duress I've been known to put on a suit and tie. I'd rather not, is all. As far as what I expect of you, I'd just like to meet you somewhere for dinner, spend a little time with you, maybe see if we do have anything in common or not."

"Meet you?" Jenna said faintly, her head swimming. "I don't know...." She looked at Nancy, who was gesturing wildly and mouthing something that could have been either "Go!" or "No!" "All right," Jenna said distractedly into the phone, "I guess that sounds okay." Nancy gave her a triumphant smile and a thumbs-up sign. Jenna grimaced ruefully back at her. "Uh...when and where shall I meet you?"

"How about tonight?"

"Tonight?" Nancy was nodding vigorously. Jenna said, "I don't know—hold on just a minute...."

"It's okay," Nancy said in a loud whisper, "I have to work until closing tonight anyway. I was going to suggest a late movie. This is even better. You can tell me all about it. *Go.*"

Jenna uncovered the mouthpiece and said calmly, "Tonight will be fine."

"Good." The word was drawn out, a purr of satisfaction. "You're where—Morro Bay? Meet me halfway—do you know a place called Smoky Joe's, in Shell Beach?"

She didn't, so he told her the freeway exit and gave her directions. "Seven o'clock okay?"

Jenna nodded, then belatedly remembered to say it into the phone. "Seven's fine."

"Well, okay, I'll see you tonight."

"Yes…all right…bye." When Jenna hung up the phone her heart was beating like a jackhammer. She swiveled on the stool and reached with a shaking hand for the coffee mug Nancy had just filled for her. "Oh, boy," she said with an explosion of unleashed breath. "What have I done?"

When Nate put the phone down he was sweating. The conversation hadn't gone quite the way he'd planned it, but on the whole he didn't think he'd done too badly. At least, he'd managed to convince the lady to see him again.

He felt like he was in about the seventh inning of a no-hitter.

"Did I just hear you makin' a date for tonight?" his housekeeper asked him on her way through his study with a broom and a dustpan. She'd been sweeping off the back porch—she liked to take the shortcut from the kitchen through his office and he'd given up trying to get her to change her route to suit his privacy. Twyla Foggett had her own way of doing things. She'd spent most of her youth on the rodeo circuit, till her husband, Tom, retired with one too many broken bones. She still wore her hair in a strawberry-blond beehive and chain-smoked cigarettes. Tom, in spite of his gimpy legs and beer belly, was still one of the best calf ropers Nate had ever seen and regularly took top honors in the local team-roping competitions. He and Twyla had never had any children, which probably explained why they'd adopted Nate.

"You're gonna have to hop to it, aren't you?" Twyla said, squinting at him as she lighted up another cigarette. "If you're gonna get to that hospital in L.A. and back and still meet your girlfriend at seven."

"Oh, shoot," Nate said, snapping his fingers. "I forgot all about that." He thought for a minute. "Is Tom around?"

"He and Charlie took the Bronco down to the south pasture to check on those heifers that're due to calve. Left just about ten minutes ago."

"Hmm, okay, they might still be in the car. Listen, see if you can get ahold of Tom on the phone for me, will you? Tell him I'm going to be needing the plane as soon as he can get it ready. And then call Santa Monica and tell them I'm coming." Nate was heading for the bathroom, already hauling his shirt up over his head.

"Want me to have a car meet you at the airport?" Twyla asked in her Gravel Gertie voice.

"Lord, no." Nate paused in his bedroom doorway to think about it. "See if you can get me a rental car, I guess. Something simple—a small pickup, maybe. I'm damned if I'm going to go see a bunch of sick kids in a limo."

"Nancy, why did you do that?" Jenna asked weakly, taking a drink of black coffee as if it might restore her failing nerve.

"Do what?"

"Tell me to go out with him!"

"Because you were going to wimp out," Nancy said reasonably. "Admit it. You would have said thanks but no thanks like the good, sensible person you are—"

"Sensible! Nancy, I have just made an assignation with a biker I met in a bar. That's not sensible, that's insane! And you—you *encouraged* me. Some friend you are!"

"Balderdash," Nancy said, a quaint expression she'd no doubt picked up from one of the British novels that were her passion. "You aren't going to have an affair with the man. All you're going to do is meet him for dinner on neutral ground. What's the harm in that? On the contrary, your cheeks are pink and your eyes sparkling.... Tell me the truth—have you once thought of Jack Remington since you picked up that telephone? *Right*. So go—have a nice little adventure. Just use good sense, that's all. Don't go anyplace where you'll have to be alone with him, don't let him in your car and for God's sake, don't get on his motorcycle!''

"Oh my stars," Jenna said faintly, resting her coffee cup against her forehead.

And suddenly for some reason she was thinking of her parents. Though it had been more than three years since the accident on an icy stretch of road in Vermont had sent the entire art world into mourning, there were times when it seemed like yesterday.

"Amazing," she said after she'd mentioned it to Nancy, setting her cup carefully on the countertop, "how much I still miss them. Considering how little I actually saw of them."

"They were your whole world," Nancy said matter-of-factly. "From the day you were born."

"Art was my world," Jenna corrected.

Nancy shrugged. "Same thing. Ian and Audrey McBride. Wow. I never saw two more dynamic personalities. They didn't just influence you, Jenna, they eclipsed you."

"Now wait, that's not—"

"Of course it's true. You inherited every bit of their talent, but your personality kind of got buried under the sheer weight of theirs, I guess. Because you have all the confidence in the world in your art, but none at all in yourself. You know you've never thought of yourself personally as anybody special—which is ridiculous. I don't see how you can look in a mirror and still think you aren't attractive. Even in college when the rest of us were out raising all kinds of hell, you were always hiding in your room with a paintbrush in your hand. I mean, so what if you were famous by the time you were twenty and we all envied you because you'd been to Paris and the White House. Where's the fun in that?''

Laughing, Jenna surrendered her coffee mug to Nancy, who refilled it and then picked up where she'd left off. "And *then*, after your parents died, when you should have been giving your own wings a try, you had to go and get involved with another irresistible force—"

"So," Jenna said, trying not to be annoyed—it was nothing, after all, that she hadn't heard Nancy say before. "You admit that Jack is irresistible."

"Of course he's irresistible," Nancy said pettishly. "He's a perfectly wonderful man. Unfortunately, he's also incomplete. He's not capable of a normal relationship—with anybody."

"I know," Jenna whispered, miserable again.

"And you deserve a complete relationship, Jen. With somebody who loves you as much as you love him. And that's why you've got to put Jack Remington behind you and get on with your life." She straightened suddenly, put down her tea cup and came across the room, waving her arms like an evangelist. "Do you realize we are now over thirty? Do you know that you and I are the only ones left out of all our friends who haven't married at least once? Do you know what our chances of ever getting married are, now that we're over thirty, according to statistics? My stars, woman, pull yourself together!"

"Don't you have to go to work?" Jenna said pointedly. But she was laughing as she got up to put her empty mug in the sink. Nancy could be an opinionated busybody at times, but her love and concern for Jenna were deep and real, and made it impossible to ever be irritated with her for long.

On the way to the stairs, Jenna paused. "Oh, God, Nan, what in the world am I going to wear?"

"A dress," Nancy answered without hesitation. "So you'll have a ready-made excuse not to get on that motorcycle! If you didn't bring one, I'll lend you one of mine."

* * *

Nate finished the autograph with a flourish. "There you go, son," he said as he handed the baseball back to the kid lying in the cranked-up hospital bed. "You take care, now."

He gave the boy's shoulder a squeeze and then, instead of moving on, for some reason he stood there, watching the way the boy turned the ball over and over in his hand, just staring at it with his lips pressed together and his eyes hot and angry. It was a big hand, Nate observed. A broad shoulder. Long, strong fingers, long, well-muscled arms...an athlete's arms.

The kid suddenly smiled. "Hey, man, I saw you pitch," he said in a soft, ghetto drawl.

"Yeah?" Nate grinned. "You must have been pretty young."

One shoulder rose and fell. "Not that young. I saw you pitch at Dodger Stadium. The year you won the Cy Young." He gave Nate a sideways look. "The Dodgers kicked your butt that night."

Nate chuckled and rubbed at the back of his neck. "Yeah, well, it happens to the best of us."

"You were pretty good," the kid conceded. "Weren't you MVP or somethin'?"

"Twice," Nate grunted, fidgeting his way toward the door. It wasn't his favorite subject and he had other kids to see, not to mention a rendezvous with a certain lady.

"Hey, man—so how many years were you in the majors?"

Again Nate looked at the kid, so dark against the stark white hospital sheets. At the big, long-fingered hands dwarfing the baseball. At the leg, fat and bulky with surgical dressings, that was elevated on top of the covers. At the defensive cant of the boy's head, the bottomless look in his eyes.

Nate walked slowly back to his bed. "Seven years."

"So why'd you quit?"

"Didn't have much choice."

"Yeah," the kid drawled, "I heard you blew your arm."

"It happens," Nate said. "That's the breaks."

The kid gave a shrug and turned his head away, toward the wall. After a moment he said very softly, "I was goin' to the pros." His voice was carefully indifferent, but Nate could see his knuckles tighten on the hand that held the baseball.

"You play ball?" Nate asked, keeping it casual.

"Nah." The look the kid gave Nate was disdainful and proud. "Basketball, man. Basketball. I was all-league three years straight. Had a scholarship and everything—full ride. I was goin' all the way, man." He snorted bitterly. "Ain't goin' nowhere now."

"That's tough," Nate said inadequately. "I'm sorry."

"Hey, it happens," the boy drawled, mocking him. "That's the breaks."

Nate was silent. He didn't blame the kid for being angry, and he knew it wasn't aimed at him. After a moment he nodded toward the bandaged leg and asked quietly, "How'd it happen?"

The boy gave a chilling laugh and turned on Nate a look that was a long way from indifference. A look so full of rage and pain it hit like a fastball in the solar plexus. "I was in the wrong place, man. I got in somebody's way." The voice was soft, almost hushed. "I was just standing there in front of my house, you know, talkin' to a couple friends. This car drives by, and the next thing I know, somebody starts shootin'. They were after somebody else.... Everybody said I was lucky." He shook his head and muttered a street obscenity, the more graphic for being so quietly spoken. "They might as well have killed me, man."

"Hey," Nate said, knowing it wasn't going to help, "come on, it's not over. You got your whole life ahead of you." Yeah, sure, Nate. The kid needed a cheerleader like he needed another broken leg.

"Yeah?" The boy hurled another gutter epithet at him and dashed angry tears from his eyes. "What do you know about it, man? Basketball was my ticket out. That bullet made hamburger meat outa my knee, so now I got nothin'. *Nothin'*, man, you dig?"

"*Wrong.*" Nate snaked a hand out and caught the kid's before he could hurl the autographed baseball across the room. "You're wrong," he growled. "Basketball isn't your ticket out, man, *this* is." He leaned over and tapped the boy's head with his knuckle. "You go to school, get your degree—that's your way out. Okay, so you forget about the damn scholarship—wait a minute...here—" He plucked the baseball from the kid's inert fingers, patted his jacket pocket for his autographing pen, scribbled on the ball and held it up right in front of the kid's wide, startled eyes. "See that? That's my home address and phone number. That's private, you understand? I don't give that out to very many people, so I'm trustin' you to keep it private. When you get out of here, you come see me and we'll work out a deal. Meanwhile, you ever need anything, you give me a call. You don't touch the gangs, the drug money, you understand me? I ever hear you've been in any kind of trouble with the law, I don't care if it's jaywalking, I'll personally break your other leg—you dig?"

The boy slowly nodded, his eyes wary and wide. His fingers curled...closed around the baseball.

"Okay then," Nate said, his voice gruff, "I'll be seein' you." He was heading for the door when the kid's soft drawl stopped him.

"Hey, Nate—Mr. Wells."

Nate turned around.

"I ain't no crybaby. But I had it all, man, you know? Girls, trophies, everybody wantin' to know me. I was *somebody*. I thought—I didn't think it was gonna end so soon. It's too *soon*, man."

Nate couldn't say anything for a moment. Then he lifted one finger and growled. "Let me tell you something, son. It doesn't make a damn bit of difference when it ends. It's always too soon."

Outside in the hallway he stopped, leaned against the wall and pressed his fingers hard against his eyelids. Then he straightened up and looked around, hoping nobody'd noticed. It sure would play hell with his image if anybody saw Nate Wells wiping away tears.

He looked at his watch and found that he was running late, as usual. Damn. He never could seem to hurry these things.

He thought about Jenna, wondered if she was the kind of woman who'd hold it against him if he kept her waiting. Then he remembered those gentle eyes of hers and he thought she'd probably forgive him, even if he couldn't tell her his reason.

It was really funny, Jenna told herself, considering how close she'd come to changing her mind about meeting this guy, to be the one stood up in the end. She supposed she ought to be relieved.

But it wasn't funny and she didn't feel relieved. She didn't know what she felt. Not surprised, really, even after replaying every moment of last night and this morning's telephone conversation with Reno over and over again in her mind. It was just the sort of thing Jack used to do, seeming so sincere about enjoying her company, about wanting to be with her, and then...

To keep herself from looking at her watch again, Jenna thrust her hands deep into the pockets of her coat and began to pace slowly along the sidewalk, hunching her shoulders against the chill. The fog was coming in, blurring the three-foot-high hot-pink neon sign above the rough-shingled roof of Smoky Joe's Café. It blurred sounds, too. The pounding of the surf was only a whisper, an intermittent concussion felt rather than heard, the foghorn a low and lonesome moan.

At the corner Jenna stopped, turned and paced slowly back to her car. Its hood and windshield were already shimmering with a fine, diamond mist.

Give it up, she said to herself. He's not coming. Go home.

The door to Smoky Joe's opened and several people came out, shrugging into jackets and exclaiming about the fog. Footsteps scraped and echoed, car doors slammed, laughter trickled away into the night. Somewhere a cat squalled once and was still.

When the new sound entered her consciousness it was almost beyond the range of human senses. A more primitive awareness picked it up and sent warnings shivering along her nerves, quickening her heartbeat and arresting her breathing. It grew steadily, became a vibration and then a growl, and finally a deep and unremitting rumble, coming closer... and closer. A light stabbed through the fog, turning it to swirling, white-gold haze. The rumble became rhythmic, a throbbing pulse-beat that seemed to resonate through Jenna's flesh and bones, like the thunder of horses' hooves.

She stood tense and still, her hands clenched tightly into fists, her heart echoing that thunder, forgetting to breathe except in meager and erratic sips. The light grew brighter, the rumble more intense. A wind whirled eddies in the fog and stirred the hair on Jenna's forehead. Out of that maelstrom of light and thunder the powerful machine and black-visaged rider appeared suddenly, as if conjured by a wizard of awesome power.

Or theatrical flare, Jenna thought sardonically, cursing her own dramatic imagination. Shaken by an ambivalence of feelings—relief, anger, excitement—she stood quite still with her hands clenched tightly inside her coat pockets, waiting for her pulse to return to normal. Strangely, it seemed to accelerate instead.

The motorcycle rolled to the curb and stopped; its engine growled and was still. The rider stood motionless astride the powerful machine, black-gloved hands on the grips, feet braced, the shield of his helmet like a mask over his face. The only sounds Jenna could hear were the tick of a cooling engine, the far -off whisper of surf and the pounding of her own heart.

Then, slowly, the rider lifted his hands, drew the helmet off and balanced it against one denim-clad thigh while he raked back his hair with his fingers. The awesome black rider disappeared; the face was the one Jenna remembered, the one she'd drawn last night in Nancy's kitchen, the one Nancy had called "dynamic." Cleft chin, solemn mouth, arrogant nose and mesmerist's eyes.... And still, instead of slowing, Jenna's heart went tripping on, like a runner stumbling helter-skelter downhill, out of control.

Reno's mouth curved in a wondering smile. "Hello, darlin'," he said softly, and shook his head. The smile slipped awry. "Why in the world are you still here?"

"I don't know," Jenna said. "I've been wondering that myself."

Four

Reno's answering chuckle was soft on the cold, misty air. Making it seem effortless, he rocked the heavy machine onto its kickstand, then came toward her, unzipping the wrists of his leather jacket, pulling off his gloves, looking her up and down with his all-seeing eyes. An arm's length away from her he stopped, reached out and touched her cheek with his fingers.

"Well, Gingerbread Lady, I'm sure glad you stayed."

His voice is like wool, Jenna thought. Soft, warm and a bit scratchy. And like wool, it made her feel too hot and slightly edgy.

She was getting ready to give him a tart rejoinder when he suddenly said, "Are you hungry?" The pure ingenuousness of the question deflated her like a worn-out balloon. The breath she was holding expired in a little whoosh, taking with it the remnants of her anger.

"Yes," she said, "I guess I am."

"Good, so'm I." Reno jerked his head toward the pink neon sign. "This place has the best barbecue in the tri-counties. You like ribs?"

"Ribs? You mean like...beef? I don't know," Jenna said doubtfully, "I don't really eat much red meat."

"Is that a moral conviction or just a matter of taste?"

"Neither. I guess..." She paused, thinking about it. "We were just always health conscious, so we ate a lot of salads and fish and things like that."

"We?" The dark gaze sharpened, intensified.

"My family," said Jenna, feeling compelled to explain. "My parents and I."

"Ah."

He put a lot into the single syllable. She answered the unspoken question with quiet dignity, but Nate noted a slight stiffening, an almost imperceptible lift of her chin. "I'm not married. I wouldn't be here if I were."

He remarked noncommittally, "You never know."

All right, so maybe he was being cynical, but traveling with a baseball team, he'd seen an awful lot of infidelity on both sides of the fence, enough to sour him on the whole subject of marriage. He'd been pretty sure she wasn't married when he'd sat down next to her at that bar, based on his instincts and the naked third finger of her left hand, but he knew from bitter experience that anything was possible. In any case, he was glad to have it cleared up. It surprised him how glad.

"Are you?" she asked, now looking a little wary herself.

"Married?" He snorted softly and shook his head. "No. Never have been."

There was a pause while her eyes searched his, looking for something—a lie, perhaps. He studied her in return, but the answers to his questions weren't there, either. What was it about her that intrigued him so? She seemed so damned mysterious, so untouchable, standing there in that trench-coat and high-heeled boots, hands in her pockets, shrouded in fog like a character in a suspense novel.

And again he felt that excitement, quickening his pulse, sharpening his senses, honing his reflexes. He knew what it was now. It was the way he'd once felt sometimes, just before taking the mound—the first inning of a big game, the late innings in a tight one, facing a tough batter, one who'd hit him hard before. *Challenge.* He hadn't realized how much he'd missed it. The lady was a mystery to him, a puzzle, an enigma as fascinating as any batter he'd ever faced, and he had an idea she could knock him right out of the box if he wasn't careful. But he knew how to be careful, and rule number one was to look relaxed. Comfortable. So he smiled as he unzipped his jacket, stowed his gloves away in an inside pocket, then said softly, "Well, that's one thing we've got in common."

He cleared his throat and lightly touched her elbow, falling into step with her when she turned. "If you're hungry and you haven't got any serious moral objections to it, we might just as well eat here. There's a Carrow's on the other side of the freeway, if you want something else, but I don't think a little beef now and then'll hurt you. Besides—you can't eat ribs with somebody and stay strangers. It's kind of like dancing, that way."

Heads turned when they walked into the restaurant. Jenna knew it wasn't on her account, but she was used to that. Heads had turned when she'd gone places with Jack, too. Women's mostly, admiring his aristocratic bearing, his elegance, his handsome head of silvery hair. But this was different. Reno was different. Men and women alike would look, take his measure . . . and give him room.

A waitress in a shiny black skirt and a white blouse that strained across the bosom and gapped between buttons showed them to a booth with red vinyl seats. She slapped down two menus and left them both with a special wink for Reno and a breezy, "There ya go, folks, have a nice evening!"

Jenna reached for a menu. Reno stopped her, touching the back of her hand with just one finger, the way he'd done in the biker's bar. And again that hand felt weighted, pinioned, incapable of movement.

"Trust me, darlin'." His voice sounded like the purr of a sleepy lion. "Last night I taught you to dance country style. Tonight I'm going to teach you to eat country style." There was a slight pause before he added, "If that's all right with you."

"Yes," Jenna murmured. "Of course."

Incredible, she thought, staring down at the strong, brown finger, the clean, crescent nail, her own slightly freckled hand. If he'd told her he planned to teach her to dance naked on tabletops she'd have acquiesced as readily. What was it about him that attracted her so?

Last night there had been an excuse, at least; she'd found herself in an unforeseen and potentially dangerous situation and he had offered her a way out of it. He had been salvation and she had clung to him as she would a log in a flood.

Tonight she was with him by her own choice. Why?

It wasn't only his looks. She'd been around attractive people all her life; certainly Jack Remington was one of the handsomest men she'd ever seen. But what was it Nancy had said when Jenna had shown her the sketch? She hadn't called him handsome or good-looking, but...*dynamic*. What was that but another word for charismatic or magnetic...or hypnotic? Perhaps, she thought in bemusement, he really was a weaver of spells, an entrancer...a wizard.

She hardly heard what he ordered for her; she was too busy studying him—covertly, she hoped. Last night his strangeness had repelled her, at first, and later he'd seemed almost like a figment of her overly vivid imagination. Now, for the first time, she wondered about him. On the telephone he'd told her he earned his living. She wondered what he did, why he didn't like to wear a suit, whether his name was really Reno and why he'd never married. She wondered what had happened to make him over an hour late meeting her. And most of all, she wondered why a man like him should be interested in her? She was so very unexciting. So ordinary...

"I called you," Reno said as soon as the waitress had gone away. "But you'd already left." His smile was off center.

Jenna looked down at her hands, cursing herself for her blush because he'd caught and so easily read the speculation in her eyes. "It's quite all right," she said stiffly. "Things come up. You needn't explain."

"Wasn't planning to." His lashes came down, briefly shuttering his eyes. And then he smiled again, effortlessly beguiling. "Sorry you had to wait, though. But I'm sure glad you did."

Jenna gazed at him steadily across her clasped hands. "Why are you glad?"

Nate caught himself shifting irritably in his seat, like a schoolboy without the answer to the teacher's question. He didn't know quite what she was asking him. "Why am I glad you waited?" he asked finally with a shrug. "Because I wanted to see you again. I told you I did. Told you I wanted to find out if we have anything in common or not." He kept his tone patient and mild, but mentally he was blaspheming and grinding his teeth. What was she driving at? Damn it, he thought, I can't talk to her. I don't know how.

She was still looking at him, cool, unblinking, unnerving. "Is that why you picked me up in that bar?"

"Is that what I did? Pick you up?" He made a sibilant sound of frustration and looked away from her for a moment. Damn it, he was used to women who flirted and flounced and hung all over him—or else got all tensed-up and tongue-tied in his presence. He didn't know what to do with one as quiet and blunt-spoken as she was. He didn't know what to make of a woman who made no effort whatsoever to sell herself, who hung back and made him do all the work.

And yet—he knew she was attracted to him. He could feel it. He'd felt it last night when she touched him; he'd seen it just now in her eyes.

"Darlin'," he said softly, "I just thought you looked like somebody who could use a friend."

Her eyes got that confused look he remembered. Her mouth opened, but before she could say anything the waitress plunked a basket of garlic bread and a pile of paper napkins on the table between them. And after that things got busy; the service at Smoky Joe's was fast and efficient. Conversation gave way to the stiff, fragmented commentary that fills in the gaps between visits by waitresses and busboys—awkward silences, meaningless chitchat, nervous smiles.

When things settled down again, Jenna slipped out of her trenchcoat, turning down Nate's offer to take it for her and leaving it kind of tucked down behind her as if, he couldn't help but think, she wasn't sure how long she planned to stay. She was wearing a peasant skirt and a blouse made out of some gauzy kind of material, with long, full sleeves and an elastic neckline that looked as if it might be meant to be worn off the shoulders. It didn't suit her, somehow, and she didn't seem comfortable with it. Her hands kept straying to the edge of the neckline, as if she didn't quite trust it to stay where it belonged.

Nate's eyes kept straying to the edge of the neckline, too, drawn there by the nervous movement of her fingers, but lingering for other reasons. Like the way the tanned place in the middle of her chest, where the sun would touch most often, only emphasized the creamy paleness farther down. And the way the ends of her hair just brushed the tops of her shoulders, tickling and teasing her skin when she moved, making his fingertips tingle with envious urges.

She made a small throat-clearing sound, and he realized that she hadn't missed the direction his eyes—and his thoughts—were taking. Her skin changed subtly, growing dusky under his gaze. He wondered if she was still thinking of him as a fox, just biding his time, waiting for the tasty morsel to fall into his mouth. The idea that she might be doing so bothered the hell out of him.

He racked his brain, trying to think of something to say or do that might help to break the ice. Last night there had been the music and the dancing, but tonight . . .

"Oh, my God," Jenna said, "that's not all for us—" A serving cart was being rolled up alongside their booth. Smiling serenely at Jenna's dismay, the waitress placed a huge platter heaped high with barbecued beef ribs, cole slaw, country-style beans and salsa on the table. Jenna stared at Reno over the mountain of food. "—Is it?"

He chuckled. "Don't worry about it. Hell, it's mostly bones. Go on," he said encouragingly when she still sat there looking helpless, "dig in, darlin'. Don't worry about your table manners. That's what the napkins are for—and those little towel things, there."

"Oh, dear," Jenna said faintly, picking up the foil-wrapped packet. She put it down again and picked up a fork instead. After a moment she put that down, too, and to her own surprise emitted a bubble of laughter. Nancy would have called it a giggle. "I feel like an idiot. I don't know where to begin."

Amusement gave his eyes a warming sheen and tilted the fan of creases at their corners. "I don't know about you," he said in his lion's purr, "but I'm going to start like this." And so saying, he shook out an oversized napkin and tucked it into the front of his shirt. The effect was unexpectedly funny. While Jenna was laughing over that and before she had any idea what he was about, he'd shaken out another napkin and reached across the table to tuck it into the neckline of her blouse.

Her laughter died in a gulp of surprise; breathing was suspended; her heart knocked once, twice, three times against the backs of his fingers.

"There you go, darlin'...." He withdrew his hand and sat back, leaving Jenna speechless and shaken.

It wasn't so much the fact that he'd touched her in that casually intimate way, although it had been surprise enough, coming from someone she barely knew. What unnerved her more, though, was her reaction to that touch. How could

ordinary human flesh produce such a sensation? she wondered, remembering last night and that first contact between her fingertips and Reno's bare arm, the way it seemed
to involve her whole body, like a jolt of electricity or some
strange and powerful drug. People were always talking
about "chemistry," about "electricity" but it really wasn't
like either of those things. It was something different and
quite unique.

Dear God, she thought, half amused, half appalled. Am
I really so needy? Was she so hungry for physical demonstrations of affection, after prolonged association with Jack
Remington, that she was in danger of coming unglued over
a man's—any man's—touch?

What a disgusting idea. She would have to guard dili-
gently against making a fool of herself.

And right on cue her imagination, always in top form at
times like this, gave her a vivid and farcical vision of herself leaping onto the back of Reno's motorcycle and speeding off with him into the sunset, hurling articles of clothing
into their dusty wake....

Nate watched the emotions play across Jenna's face with
fascination and frustration. Like images seen through a
fogged window, he couldn't quite make sense of them. First
the surprise, which was clear enough and understandable;
and then the faint but unmistakable signs of sexual response—so far so good. But after that he was on shakier
ground. There was confusion, fear and even, he could have
sworn, a hint of laughter. And finally the look he remembered best, the look that never failed to ignite the banked
embers of desire in his belly: that wicked little spark of
daring.

"Now, here's what you do," he said, pulling them both
back to the business at hand with great effort. "You pick up
a bone—that's right, with your fingers—and you hold it like
this."

In that vein he instructed and she followed, and watching her, Nate knew that he'd never in his life seen anything
so beautifully and unconsciously sensual as the way Jenna

dealt with that meal. If she'd done it on purpose it would have been earthy, ribald and funny, perhaps like the eating scene in *Tom Jones*. But because she so obviously hadn't a seductive or licentious thought in her head, it was something else entirely. Whatever it was, he couldn't take his eyes off her. Strong white teeth . . . lips glazed and sticky with barbecue sauce . . . the frown of consternation in her eyes just before she closed them with a small, surrendering sigh.

At first she wanted to reach for a napkin after every delicate and tentative bite. "You'll go through every napkin in the place if you keep doing that," he told her. "Relax, no one's lookin'." Which wasn't altogether true. He, for one, was deriving a great deal of pleasure from watching her tongue try to steal barbecue sauce from her lips before anyone saw it; from the way she looked at her fingers with dismay, the way a child might, just before she drew them, one by one and with obvious relish, into her mouth.

She paused when she caught him watching her and made a prim little throat-clearing sound. "This is quite good," she said, her eyes shining with a mixture of embarrassment and fun. "What do I do with the bone when I'm finished—toss it over my shoulder and call for a flagon of ale?"

Nate gave a bark of surprised laughter. "The lady behind you might get a little bit upset," he said in a low voice. "And the guy with her looks big and mean. Maybe you'd best just put it here, on this platter, seeing as how I seem to have left my sword and armor outside." But it tickled him that she'd picked up on the medieval connection, since it was her talk about knights and armor that had made him think of bringing her here in the first place. That was some imagination she had, to put *him* in shining armor. No, wait—not shining; she'd said *black*. The Black Knight. Which was probably a lot closer to the mark, he thought, squirming with unheralded pangs of guilt.

"Oh my goodness," Jenna said much later, eyeing the platter of vanquished bones, "I can't believe we ate that. What do you suppose they do with all these bones? This must be a dog's idea of heaven."

"Well," Reno drawled, tearing open one of the little foil packets of finger wipes, "mine'll be happy, I know... there you go, darlin'." He handed her a finger wipe and set about unfolding his own.

Jenna leaned eagerly forward, forgetting the mess her hands and face were in. "You have a dog?"

"Several."

"Really? What kind?"

"Just dogs." He shrugged, then focused on her with narrowed, probing eyes. "You like dogs?"

Now it was she who shrugged, trying to keep from her voice a wistfulness that had caught her unawares. "We always—I've always traveled so much...." She smiled suddenly. "My grandparents had cats."

"Yeah," Reno muttered, "I've got a few of those, too. Here, hold still a minute...."

Once again she was caught, suspended between breaths, between heartbeats, as he leaned forward, briefly touched her chin as if to steady or perhaps reassure her, then scrubbed at her cheek with the moist, sweet-smelling tissue. Hold still? She couldn't have moved if her life depended on it. His eyes held her entranced... bewitched... helpless.

"There you go—I think that's got it." He took way his hand, slowly. His gaze remained.

"Umm, cats..." Jenna mumbled, but she'd forgotten what it was she'd meant to say. A shiver rippled through her.

"Hey," Reno's voice came softly, from far away. "What do you say we get out of here?"

Get out of here...and go where? *Don't go anyplace where you'll have to be alone with him....* There was a little silence, while Nancy's warnings echoed in Jenna's head, and then Jenna said, "All right," knowing full well that it was a doorway, of sorts. A doorway leading to an exciting, possibly dangerous unknown.

Outside again, shivering in her trenchcoat, she was almost grateful for the fog. For one thing, it gave her an excuse for the shivering, though she knew it was more from nerves than the chill. And it shrouded everything—herself with her collar turned up and a strand of hair wafting across her damp cheek, and Reno beside her, black leather jacket wet with mist and gleaming like armor—in a veil of fantasy. None of it felt real. And because it didn't seem real, she could allow herself to be swept along in it, as in a dream.

In a dream, you didn't have to make choices.

Even the fog had a rosy, dreamlike glow, from the pink neon sign overhead. All sounds were muffled except their own, and those seemed unnaturally loud—the scrape of shoes on sidewalk, the rustle of cloth against her legs, the sigh of a breath, the muted thunder of heartbeats, the whisper of leather . . . so near. So very near.

Reluctantly, fearfully and yet somehow compelled, like someone investigating noises in the dark, she turned her head to look at Reno. And found him looking back at her, his eyes quiet, his windswept head haloed in mist. The shivers inside her grew sharper and tighter, but she didn't look away.

Black Knight, she wondered, or black magic? Either way, she was surely caught in his spell.

"Feel like dancing?" Nate suddenly asked her, his voice too loud in that strange quiet. "It's Friday night. There's a place not too far from here that'll have country music. No bluegrass, and it's apt to be a little rowdy, but it's okay for dancing. We can walk it, if you want to, or you can hop on the back—" He almost laughed out loud at the look on her face—like Little Red Ridinghood meeting the wolf in the woods.

"You mean . . . ride?" she said, her voice squeaking a little. "On your m-motorcycle? Oh—well, I can't, can I? I mean, I'm not dressed for it."

This time he did chuckle—he couldn't help it, she was so damned easy to read. "Sure," he said easily, "you're wearing a full skirt, aren't you? No problem. Just tuck it in around your legs so it doesn't get on the pipes—hell, I know ladies who drive these things to work in business suits."

Then, putting his arm around her shoulders, he bent down to whisper in her ear. "Darlin', if you want an excuse to stay off a bike, the best thing to wear is something tight. And long. Slinky, maybe midcalf or ankle length, you know what I mean?" She opened her mouth like she wanted to deny it was what she'd had in mind, but didn't say anything. "Of course," Nate added thoughtfully, "even then you could still ride if you don't mind showin' a little leg."

She looked so dismayed he decided to stop teasing her. He laughed and gave her shoulders a squeeze, then let his arm drop away. "Come on," he said gently, "we'll walk."

They walked slowly and in silence, moving in and out of the milky aureoles cast by street lamps and lighted windows, their footsteps crunching in unison, the surf like a gossip's whispers in the distance.

After a while Nate said casually, "You know, sometime soon you're going to have to make up your mind whether I'm your knight or that fox you're so afraid of. You know that, don't you?"

He said it as if it didn't matter much to him one way or the other, because it was his way never to let on when he wasn't altogether sure of himself. When you didn't have your best stuff, that was when you wanted to go out there with the iron jaw and the eagle eye and drill the first pitch high and inside, just to give the guy at the plate something to think about.

But it did matter to him. It surprised him how much.

"Oh," she said, walking along with her hands in her coat pockets and her head down, hair falling like a curtain across her cheeks, "I already know what you are."

Suspense tightened his chest. "Yeah?"

"Oh, yes. A knight. Definitely."

Now, perversely, though it was the answer he wanted from her, he felt guilty about it. He halted abruptly and blurted, "Why?" Then softened the harshness of it with a shrug and an offhand, "Just out of curiosity..."

She stopped, too, head tilted, thinking about it. "Well, partly because of the way you look." The smile she gave him was elusive and shy. "You know, with the helmet, the bike and...everything. There's something so—" She stopped and shook her head as if her thoughts dismayed her, then turned to walk on, continuing in the same thoughtful way. "And because you came to my rescue in that bar."

"You didn't need rescuing," Nate said flatly.

"But I would have, if you hadn't—"

He shook his head, silently calling himself a fool and wondering why he felt this need, all of a sudden, to come clean. "No, you wouldn't. Sure, they'd have tried to hit on you, but all you'd have to do is say no, and they'd have left you alone."

She'd stopped again, in a pool of swirling white-gold mist beneath a street lamp, looking puzzled. "You knew them? Those two bikers?"

"Yeah," Nate said. He took a deep breath. "Hawk and Willie are pretty harmless, if you want to know the truth."

"You mean . . . you lied to me?"

"Well . . ."

"You lied," Jenna asserted, more in surprise than outrage, slowly pulling strands of hair away from one damp cheek. When he didn't answer, she shot at him point blank, "Why did you do that?"

"Well, hell," he blustered, the more defensive for knowing he was guilty, "I knew the minute you walked in that I wanted to talk to you. And I could see you weren't feeling good about being there. What would you have done if I'd just sat down and started talking to you?"

"So." She took a big breath and lifted her chin, as if she were preparing to let him have it. "You were doing the same thing they were? Hank and . . . what's—"

"Hawk. Hawk and Willie. And no, I wasn't. I told you, I thought you looked like you could use a friend."

"But you just said—"

"Lady," Nate growled, "Hawk and Willie weren't what was snappin' at your heels when you walked into that place."

They stood face-to-face, glaring at each other. They hadn't been shouting, but the words were sharp and intense, and stung like buckshot.

"So," Jenna said after a minute, "all of that—you coming over to me, dancing with me, walking me to my car and then calling me up and inviting me to meet you for dinner—all that was because you figured I needed a *friend*?"

Nate wondered how a person could look so proud and so vulnerable at the same time. Her eyes were hard and unflinching and her chin was up, but her mouth had a precarious look to it. He had an urge to draw his thumb across her lower lip and see if he could make her smile again, but he knew that in some obscure way he'd hurt her and that right now she'd probably jerk away from his touch. So he stuck his hands in his jacket pockets to curb his impulses and drawled softly, "Only the first part."

She didn't seem to hear him, but went on in tones of bald skepticism, "And you don't want ... anything from me."

"No," Nate murmured, "I don't want anything *from* you."

The subtle emphasis was lost on her; the only reply was a soft hiss of disbelief.

He touched her shoulder and said gently, "Darlin', just what is it you think I want?"

Her chin rose another notch. "Correct me if I'm wrong, but generally when a man picks up a woman in a bar, isn't it because he wants to go to bed with her?"

She lobbed that at him like a hand grenade, expecting to shock him with her boldness, perhaps, or maybe embarrass him in his lie. She looked disconcerted when he only laughed.

"Darlin', is that what's worrying you? You figure I'm planning to take you to bed?"

Five

Her face was pale in the ghostly light, with fine beads of moisture dusting her skin like sequins on satin. She didn't look quite real, and it surprised Nate when he touched her cheek to discover that it was warm.

He said softly, "I wouldn't have brought it up for a while yet if you hadn't asked, but since you have, let's get it out of the way. Do I want to take you to bed? Hell, yes, I do—what man wouldn't?"

She gave a slight, involuntary start, which he might have missed if he hadn't been touching her and if he hadn't seen the shock register in her eyes. But he didn't miss it, and the rest of what he'd planned to say zapped right out of his mind. For a long time he just stood there looking at her, feeling her warmth against the back of his fingers, listening to the uneven whisper of her breathing while realization and understanding spread through him like the light of a rising sun.

The lady truly didn't know how beautiful she was.

Beautiful? Well, he hadn't thought so himself, he remembered, not at first. But he did now. Oh, yes, he did now. And it was his awareness of that fact as much as her lack of it that both sobered and silenced him.

Up to now, beautiful women had never been much of a mystery to him, and seldom much of a challenge, either. But this one was different. She reminded him of one of those puzzle boxes, where you finally get it open only to find another one equally baffling inside.

So that aloofness of hers was nothing more than shyness, and her confusion was due to lack of confidence. It seemed unfathomable to him. How could she not know? Hell, he thought disgustedly, she was probably just putting on an act of some kind. Most of the women he'd known were good at that.

But the answer to that was obvious, even to him. The confusion was in her eyes, plain to see. He could feel the questions teetering on the edge of each and every breath she took. She really *didn't* know. Godalmighty, where had she been, in a box? For her to be so totally unaware of her own appeal seemed to him to require an innocence impossible in this day and age, the kind of innocence he didn't believe in anymore and that probably never had existed except in myths and fairy tales.

Fairy tales? Like the ones about gingerbread ladies and knights in armor? In one rare moment of fancy, Nate wondered if Jenna were some kind of time traveler, stranded in the wrong age. *Lost lady*...

She was getting to him, no doubt about it.

There wasn't any mystery about the way she affected him physically. She was soft flesh and warm blood, and her cheek was vibrant against his fingers, making him itch to touch her in a variety of interesting and exciting ways. But for some reason he was suddenly aware of the tenuousness of that contact, of the fragility of the moment, of the need to go carefully...oh, so carefully. What should he say to her? What should he do now? Such uncertainty was new to him, but damn it, he'd never met anyone like her before!

All his experience, his intelligence, his common sense were telling him to go easy, to take it slow with this lady. But there was something else—instinct, maybe. It was the feeling he used to get when he'd shake off his catcher's signs and decide to go with his best pitch against all logic and baseball's well-calculated odds. He'd never regretted going with that gut feeling yet, but there was always a first time. His heart was beating fast and hard as he slowly uncurled his fingers and cradled Jenna's cheek in the palm of his hand, as he drew his thumb across the satiny softness of her lips, then quickly lowered his head to catch their involuntary parting.

The unexpected taste of her, just that small, sweet sip of her breath, hit him in the chest like a slug of neat whisky and spread a familiar heat all the way to his belly and beyond. His heart gave a great surge. He drew back a little, closed his eyes and released a gust of silent, rueful laughter.

"Oh, yeah," he murmured, desire thickening his voice, "I want to make love to you, sure I do." Again he felt her shocked recoil, but his fingers were already pushing past the cool edge of her ear, into the dense thicket of her hair. He held her there so that his lips just touched the words to her cheek, the contact so light it made his nerve endings tingle. "But...I'm not going to. Not for a while yet. Not until you want me to, darlin', and tell me you do."

But it occurred to him even as he said it that for a woman like Jenna to tell him of her wanting, she'd have to trust him first. Trust him completely. And she didn't, not yet. So he reluctantly pulled away, just far enough to look at her, and added with a smile, "That's a promise. And now we've got that settled and out of the way, are you still afraid to kiss me?"

"I'm not afraid," Jenna said, sounding faintly affronted.

"Well," he growled, "that's good...."

No, Jenna wasn't afraid. It's a dream, she told herself. Everything that was happening to her seemed somehow inevitable, beyond her control. But still...it had been so long since anyone had kissed her—really kissed her—that in the split second before Reno's lips touched hers, she wondered if she would even know what to do.

And then she felt the warmth of his breath again, the silkiness of his mouth—not such a surprise this time—and an exciting new texture, the slight roughness of beard stubble just under the edge of his lower lip. Inside her chest, a small flower of warmth blossomed, making her want to smile. Her lips parted and softened; she felt the intimate intrusion of his tongue, surprising in its gentleness, unanticipated in its effect on her. Her stomach suddenly knotted and coiled like a spring being wound too tightly. She gasped, her hands clutched blindly, found the clammy suppleness of leather and held on. Reno raised his head, his big, strong hands coming to support her elbows, and she was left holding on to his arms, staring at the base of his throat and swallowing repeatedly.

Okay, she thought, dazed. That went well. Her legs were shaking, but she hadn't fallen apart, she wasn't going to make a fool of herself, and it was obvious that being hopelessly in love with Jack Remington hadn't affected her ability to respond physically to another man. She felt a surge of exhilaration, almost of triumph. Maybe Nancy was right, the human heart *was* resilient. Maybe all it needed was a healer's touch. Or a wizard's. *Merlin's touch.*

Reno's dark eyes were watchful, as if he were waiting for her to say something.

But her thoughts were too complicated for words; instead she gave a soft ironic laugh and shook her head. It seemed to be enough response for Reno, because he laughed, too, and put his arm lightly around her shoulders, and they walked on together through fine, swirling mist.

"Well," he said a few minutes later, "this is the place." He'd halted before a door flanked by outlines of cowboy hats and cactus plants in pink and green neon on silvered wood siding. The door was open, and the throbbing beat of a bass guitar was pumping waves of music and laughter out into the street. The smells of beer and cigarette smoke mixed with the fog, giving it texture and density, like soup.

"Loud," Reno commented, peering through the doorway into the murky cavern beyond.

Jenna nodded. She was remembering the bikers' bar and Ernie Rose's band and the way the music had touched her. The way Reno had touched her.

He was looking at her, his smile wry. "I'm not sure I'm in the mood for this. How 'bout you?"

"No," she said, "not really." She didn't know whether she was relieved or disappointed. The music wasn't the same, and she usually didn't like noisy, crowded, smoky places, but—

"You want to just walk some more?"

Jenna nodded, staring at the front of Reno's leather jacket, remembering vividly the way his smooth bare arms had held her, the way his body's heat and smell had enveloped her. And she knew suddenly that she *was* disappointed because what she wanted more than anything in the world was to dance with Reno again. To have him hold her that way again.

"Yes," she murmured, "that would be nice."

She couldn't tell him what she really wanted, not in a million years. Oh, she thought desperately, how terrible it was to need someone! She always seemed to be at the mercy of emotions and impulses she wasn't strong-willed or experienced enough to handle, first with Jack, and now—Oh, God, she thought, if Reno knew how vulnerable she was . . . what would he do?

"Hell, yes, I want to make love to you."

"You cold?"

She gave a start, then shrugged to hide it. "Just a little," she said through chattering teeth. "If we walk, it will probably be okay."

Reno nodded and put his arm around her shoulders again.

"But I'm not going to . . . until you want me to."

They walked along the sea wall, listening to the muffled boom of the surf, the clang of buoys, the moan of a fog horn, the scrape of their footsteps. Jenna thought about

Nancy's warnings. *Whatever you do, don't...* And here she was, all alone in the night with a long-haired, tattooed stranger she'd met in a biker's bar, a man who'd just told her flat-out he intended to take her to bed, eventually. But his arm was a comforting weight, his body big and warm beside her, and she knew that against all odds, she felt safe, even protected. How could that be? It didn't make sense.

"Darlin'," Reno said, "what are you thinking about so hard?" When she looked up at him, he rubbed a knuckle gently down the middle of her forehead. "It's got you furrowed up like a washboard."

Jenna gave a breathy laugh and answered honestly, "I was just thinking...about what you said a while ago. About wanting to—" she took a deep breath "—to go to bed with me."

"Yeah?"

She waited for him to say more, and when he didn't, she drew another chestful of air she didn't really need and let it out again. This kind of frankness was new to her, and oddly exciting. "And...what you said about my needing a friend."

"Uh-huh."

"Well," she demanded, frustrated with him for not reading her mind, for not saving her from having to formulate a question when she wasn't sure what it was she wanted to know, "which one is it?"

She felt his body give a slight jerk, but whether with laughter or surprise she couldn't tell. He stopped walking and looked down at her. "Does it have to be one or the other?"

Jenna spent a moment or two pondering that idea, much as she'd earlier pondered the best way to attack a mountain of messy barbecued ribs. Then she shrugged and said, "I knew someone...once. He always insisted that it did."

"Oh, yeah?" Reno pounced on that like a hawk on a mouse, his eyes sharp and inquisitive.

"Yes." She drew a careful breath. "He always said that . . . sex spoils a good friendship. He wouldn't—" She stopped and looked away. "Never mind."

Reno's fingers touched her chin, pulling her back to him. "Let me tell you something, darlin'. I've known people, too, and there were a lot of things they told me, most of which I'd just as soon not remember."

His voice was soft and lazy—the lion's purr—but there was something in it that made Jenna remember all the things she'd wondered about him and realize how little she knew. Her gaze flew upward to his face, but it was in shadow.

He lifted a strand of hair that had blown across her cheek. "But this right here—this is just you and me. Nobody else. We make up the rules as we go along. Whatever feels right."

The soft voice stopped, and Reno's fingers began to talk for him. Clever, eloquent fingers . . . brushing her cheek, stroking the strand of hair behind her ear, tracing the curve of her ear with their tips. She watched him, mesmerized, while his fingers pushed into her hair and began to move on the base of her skull in slow, massaging circles. Her eyelids grew heavy.

"Hey," he whispered, suddenly commanding. "Come 'ere, pretty lady."

She swayed forward, lifting her face for his kiss. It seemed so right this time. So easy. His mouth was already becoming familiar to her. She welcomed its warmth with a little sigh of pleasure, curving her lips against his in a smile.

Reno smiled, too. A low chuckle rumbled through him, full of masculine confidence and mastery. The sound awoke astonishing responses in Jenna, primitive responses, seemingly untouched by modern feminist ideology or currently accepted attitudes of sexual equality. She heard another sound, soft and uniquely feminine, an acknowledgment of mastery and a surrender to it. She was shocked to realize that it had come from her.

There was a subtle shifting and tightening. Reno's body arched, his mouth covered hers, lips sensual and sure, his tongue's demand—and message—unmistakable. Even with her limited knowledge Jenna knew that this kiss was a simulation of sexual possession, shockingly graphic, intensely and deliberately erotic. The way his mouth controlled her, the firm but gentle pressure of his lips opening her to receive the first penetration of his tongue; the way his moist heat filled her, taking up all the space inside her, so that her whole body rocked to the slow, rhythmic strokes of his tongue....

Heat exploded through her. She was a furnace inside her trenchcoat; she wanted to tear it off, but there was no strength at all in her muscles. If it hadn't been for Reno's hands cradling the back of her head, and hers holding on to his belt for dear life, she would have fallen. And still the invasion of her mouth intensified, deepened until she felt it in every part of her, tingling in her hands and feet, pumping through her veins, throbbing low and deep in her body and between her thighs. Her breath began to come in pants, then in whimpers.

And then Reno made another primitive sound, something like a groan, the sound of a strong man torn in two. He began to withdraw from her, not all at once, but slowly, regretfully...easing away and coming back again and yet again with soft, soothing kisses...and finally folding her close and settling his chin upon her hair, breathing hard. She felt the powerful ripple of his throat as he swallowed.

"Hey, are you okay?" he asked in a quiet voice.

Jenna wasn't, and she had an idea he knew that very well, so she didn't answer. She felt weak and ravaged. She felt like a car left in neutral with its motor racing, overheating, ready to explode. She felt angry and frightened. She felt like crying.

Damn him anyway. Damn him for stripping her naked, for exposing her secret vulnerabilities. Damn him for making her know how hungry she was, when she'd tried so hard to make herself believe she didn't care, she didn't *need*...she didn't *want*. Damn Reno for making her want *him*.

"Until you want me to, darlin', and tell me you do."

Oh, God, she thought. And wasn't that what she'd just done? She wanted him, no doubt about it, and by her actions had surely told him so. Did that mean...? But she couldn't—he hadn't meant—she wasn't ready! She pushed away from him and looked up into his face.

"I'm fine," she croaked earnestly. "Just fine."

Reno gave a funny little laugh and stretched gingerly, as if trying to ease cramped muscles. "Well, I'm glad you are, darlin'," he said dryly, "because I'm sure as hell not. I'm damned uncomfortable, if you want to know the truth." He moved away from her, shaking his head and muttering. "My own damn fault. That was a dumb thing to do. I don't know what I was thinkin' about.... I've got to walk this off."

Jenna couldn't have walked if her life had depended on it. She stood where she was, a cold wind stirring through her hair, cooling her cheeks, making her nose run.

I don't understand this, she thought as shudders wracked her body. What did he want from her? What was he doing to her? No man had ever kissed her the way he'd just kissed her. No man had ever talked to her the way he talked to her. And now that she'd all but thrown herself at his feet, he was walking away. She'd never felt so confused.

But if she didn't understand Reno, she understood herself even less. She wanted him—and she didn't. Wanting him—a stranger, a man she'd met in a bar and barely knew—made her feel ashamed. She couldn't deny the things she felt when he touched her, the hunger that burned inside her—yes, even now—but those feelings profoundly embarrassed her. And at the same time she wanted to shout at someone, *Damn it, it's time!* She was almost thirty years old. She'd spent her whole life wrapped up in her work—all her energy, youth and passion—it had all gone into her painting. And then she'd fallen in love. Classically, passionately, stupidly head-over-heels in love—a walking, talking cliché! Unfortunately it had been with a man who couldn't love her back.

Now it seemed there was no painting left in her, or love, either. But she was still a woman, damn it! She was almost thirty years old and she was lonely and hungry, and it was *time*.

Reno had stopped and was looking quizzically at her, holding out his hand. "Come on, Gingerbread Lady." His voice was gentle, and hinted at a smile. "I won't eat you."

A dozen tart answers to that remark flitted through Jenna's head, but she didn't say anything. After a moment she gave him her hand.

They walked in silence while her shivers gradually subsided and her hand grew warm, wrapped in Reno's strong grasp. After a while she felt his head turn, and then the prolonged and discomfiting probe of his eyes.

"You're a sweet and very sexy lady, you know that?" he said in a soft, guttural voice.

Sexy? Jenna's hand jerked reflexively, but he held on to it. "Yeah, you are." He drew a deep, sighing breath. "And right now I want you so bad I ache all over."

She opened her mouth, but there was absolutely nothing she could think of to say. *Sexy?* She felt herself filling up with a sweet and wild confusion....

She could feel Reno's gaze on her again, caressing as the touch of his fingers, soft as a whisper. "And I like you, sexy lady."

Startled, she looked up at him. But he was already deep in his own thoughts and so missed the wonder and revelation of hers clearly written on her face. It's so simple, she thought. And it explained so much about herself and the way she was behaving. Because the truth was, she liked him, too.

"I imagine," Reno said as they walked along, his head tilted thoughtfully, his big, warm hand surrounding hers, "there are some people who can't manage it—the sex and friendship thing. I've known a few." He glanced down at her. "And then there are people who have to have the friendship for the sex to be any good at all. That's you, darlin'." Jenna stared back at him, mesmerized by his voice, his nearness. He took a deep breath. "That's why it was stupid of me to kiss you like that, and why I'm coolin' us both down now. Because I want it good between us. You understand?''

She shook her head. Nate sighed. "Some women..." he said, and then stopped. He didn't know how to explain it to her without making himself sound like something he wasn't. He didn't know how to tell her about the women he'd known—and there'd been a lot of them—who'd wanted nothing from him but what was in his pants and whatever thrill it was they seemed to get from making it with a big-name star—the glamour, the excitement—he'd never really understood it. That's all they'd cared about, and not necessarily in that order. They hadn't given a damn about who Nate Wells really was, and after a while he'd gotten to where he hadn't given a damn about them, either. It was the part of his former life he didn't miss—the waking up in strange cities, in look-alike hotel rooms with look-alike strangers in his arms and a cold, hollow feeling in the pit of his stomach. He'd gotten sick of that game long before he'd bowed out of the one that paid his salary, and it was a sickness it had taken him a long time to shake.

"Never mind," he said softly. He carried Jenna's hand to his mouth and brushed his lips across her knuckles, not wanting to look at her because he was certain he knew what he'd see in her eyes. If he wanted to, he could take her to bed now, tonight, as easily and as quickly as he'd taken so many others back in the days when he'd still been playing the game.

But this woman wasn't like those others. For one thing, he was positive she had no idea who he was, so if she wanted him—and she did, probably against her own better judgment—he knew it sure as hell wasn't because of his name. And though the fact that she did want him made him feel good, which was a nice change in itself, it also seemed to have saddled him with an unprecedented sense of responsibility. Because Jenna was different. If she didn't even know she was beautiful, he could only guess how many other things she didn't know. She wanted him, but it was upsetting her that she did, and he knew that if he took her to bed now, it wouldn't make either of them happy. It came home to him suddenly that what he'd said about Jenna needing friendship to make the sex good was true for him, as well. It always had been. He just hadn't ever met a woman he particularly wanted to be friends with, he realized as he looked down at the wisps of dark hair blowing softly against his shoulder. Until now.

"I want to see you again," Reno said brusquely when they were once more back on the sidewalk in front of Smoky Joe's. "Tomorrow. Meet me again and we'll go somewhere."

Jenna made a faint, distressed sound and whispered, "Together?"

"That's the idea." He smiled and leaned casually against his motorcycle. "It's a lot more fun that way."

"Oh, well," Jenna said helplessly. Together? But that would mean ... "I guess we could, uh ... my car, umm ..."

"Jenna ..." Reno was shaking his head, his smile gently mocking. "It scares you, doesn't it?" he said softly, with a slight movement of his head and shoulders that took in the big black Harley parked beside the curb, covered with moisture now, glistening in the light of the neon sign like the hide of a healthy animal.

"A little," Jenna admitted, her heart beating faster. "It seems ... very powerful. Dangerous." But exciting, she thought as a strange and unexpected thrill ran through her. Yes, *exciting*.

"Yeah, it's powerful," Reno drawled, watching her now with his sorcerer's eyes. "And dangerous, if you don't know how to control it. You'd have to trust me to keep you safe, I guess." Something odd was happening to his voice. It deepened, grew softer but at the same time richer, leaving Jenna without any doubt that if he ever had been, he was no longer talking about motorcycles. "You'd have to believe I know what I'm doing, that I'd never do anything to hurt you."

"Yes," Jenna whispered, her lips tingling with a sudden and vividly sensual memory. "I guess I would."

His voice persisted. "Do you believe that?"

She swallowed, and with a sense of wonder heard herself answer, "Yes. I do."

"Then come with me. Meet me tomorrow, and I'll take you for a ride."

"A . . . ride?"

He folded his arms and tilted his head back, teasing her now with his lazy drawl and self-confident smile. "Come on, Gingerbread Lady, if I didn't gobble you up tonight when I had the chance, what do you think's gonna happen in broad daylight? Aren't you the lady that walked all alone into a biker's nest? Where's your sense of adventure?" *Come on, Nate urged her silently, where is it, darlin'? I know you've got it, I've seen it in your eyes. Courage...daring...like a spark of cold blue flame.* "You must have one, or you wouldn't be here, with me, tonight."

"All right, all right!" She surrendered, feeling breathless and scared as a child on a Ferris wheel. "I'll meet you tomorrow. Where, here? And what time?" *I'm sorry, Nancy, I'm sorry, I know it's crazy.*

"Here's fine. High noon." He swung one leg across the bike in a swift and graceful motion and took the helmet from the handlebars, chuckling as he said, "Oh, and darlin'...wear pants. You'll be more comfortable."

The mocking grin, boyishly cleft chin and sorcerer's eyes abruptly disappeared, eclipsed by a dark, mirrored visor. As magically as a wizard changing his physical form, he became the warrior again, the awesome black knight, pulling on his gauntlets. The motorcycle snarled and roared to life.

Jenna's breath caught. She stood there, cemented to the spot, until Reno pointed to her car and she realized he was waiting for her to get in and start up her engine. Only when he saw her lights come on did he finally touch a gloved finger to his helmet and roar away into the night.

The fog had thinned somewhat. Jenna drove home without any trouble at all, though it was several miles before her heart ceased its futile hammering against the barrier of her ribs.

Six

Nancy was waiting up for her, of course, sitting cross-legged in the middle of the living room sofa.

"It was very interesting," Jenna said in answer to the anticipated question. "I had a good time."

The plastic-covered library edition Regency romance novel Nancy had been reading dropped with a thud onto the coffee table. "Interesting?" she said, bestowing on Jenna the skeptical glare of a born inquisitor. "Jen, you just had a date with a biker. Is that all you have to say—that it was *interesting*?"

"He was...nice," Jenna said after a moment's consideration, holding back laughter. It wasn't like her to tease, but a strange new effervescence was rising like leavening inside her.

"Nice." Nancy sat back and folded her arms across the eyelet ruffle on her nightgown, looking affronted. "Right. My dear, this is me you're talking to. You look like you just got off a thrill ride. 'Nice' doesn't put those roses in your cheeks and that look in your eyes, or make a mess of your hair like you've just been—''

"Well, he was."

Nancy sighed. "All right, so tell me—where did you go? What did you do?"

"We had dinner," Jenna said, "at a place called Smoky Joe's." She paused in the process of unbelting and unbuttoning her trenchcoat to add thoughtfully, "I don't think I've ever eaten ribs before. It was interesting. Messy, but...liberating, in a way. And then we—'' she turned quickly to lay her coat over the back of a chair, concealing her face but not the breathiness in her voice ''—we went for a walk.''

Nancy's interest quickened. "A walk! Where?"

"Just...along the street. Beside the ocean."

"Good Lord."

Jenna lifted her head, took a deep, fortifying breath and plunged. "And he kissed me. Twice. No...three times, if you count the first time, which was more like just a hello."

"And how do you feel about it?" Nancy inquired in the casually somber manner of a professional counsellor.

"I don't—'' Jenna lifted her hands and let them fall. "I don't know if I can possibly tell you how I feel. I've never felt like this before." She shifted irritably, as if the feelings were making her itch. "And anyway, words are your thing, not mine." No, not words. Her medium of expression was oil paint on canvas—acrylics or water colors in a pinch. But how would she ever paint such feelings? In cadmium yellow, she thought...and cobalt blue and dazzling titanium white. The colors of sunshine and summer.

She paced the tiny living room aimlessly, frowning with the effort of sorting out the confusion inside her. "I'm not in love," she said positively. "I know that. This isn't anything like what I felt—feel for Jack. This feels—I feel—too good, too lighthearted. Love makes you feel scared... uncertain."

"It doesn't have to," Nancy said, looking taken aback. "I don't think it should."

"It does," Jenna said flatly. "Because you know you can get hurt. But I don't feel like that. I just feel like I'm having fun. I like being with Reno. It's exciting. Everything is new, different. Nancy, I *like* him." She threw her arms out suddenly, laughing in sheer exuberance. "I guess that's what I am—I'm in *like*. Is it possible, do you think? Is there such a thing?"

"Huh," Nancy said, looking disbelieving again, and slightly disappointed. "You mean to tell me, no passion at all? With a face like that, all that charisma—"

"Oh. Well," muttered Jenna, clearing her throat, "I never said *that*."

Passion? What a pale word to describe that kiss and the way she'd responded to it. Her skin on fire, her body heavy and weak, her heart gone crazy, throbbing in strange, unsettling places...

"Passionate like..." Nancy mused, gazing into space and mercifully missing the sudden rush of heat to Jenna's face that must have illuminated her thoughts like a neon sign. "You know, that might not be a bad thing for you right now. You don't want to get involved in anything too heavy too soon. You need to give your emotions a rest. Yeah... I think passionate like is great." Having apparently decided to give her blessings and approval to the whole affair, she rearranged her legs and sat eagerly forward. "So, are you going to see him again?"

"Tomorrow," Jenna said and was instantly struck by a dampening wave of guilt. Clapping her hand over her mouth, she said, "Oh—Nancy, I'm sorry. I don't know what I was thinking of. We were going to—"

"No," Nancy said briskly, "that's all right, this is important. This is what you came up here for, after all, isn't it—to get your broken heart patched up? If this guy can do that for you, hey, listen, I'm all for it. I have things I need to do anyway, both here and at the library. I'll get caught up and we'll have all day Sunday to play."

She was sincere, Jenna knew she was sincere, but it didn't make her feel better. She began to pace again, rubbing her arms, suddenly as swamped with uncertainty as she'd been giddy with euphoria only moments ago. "I wish I had some way...but I can't even call him. I don't know where he lives or even what his name is—besides Reno." She drew an uneven breath. "I don't have to go. I could just not show up."

But the thought made her feel cold and hollow inside and shaky, as if she were suffering from some kind of delayed reaction to a brush with catastrophe.

She didn't have to go through with it. If she didn't go to meet Reno tomorrow, she'd probably never have to see him again. *Reno* ... whoever he was, with his wizard's eyes and healer's touch and his big, black, dangerous motorcycle. With his big strong hands and warm brown skin and mouth as smooth and supple as satin. She could just not show up— if she didn't answer Nancy's phone, how would he ever find her?—and by so doing, turn her back on the new and exciting—and frightening—things he had to teach her. Things like bluegrass music, Western dancing, eating barbecued ribs with her fingers. Racing the wind on the back of a motorcycle, with sun-warmed leather against her cheek and her arms locked around a powerful, muscular body.... She tried to stop there, but her mind wouldn't let her. *Do I want to make love to you? Hell, yes....* Oh, the new and exciting and frightening things he could teach her!

What would it be like to make love with Reno? Her mind gave her questions, images, impressions, but no answers. She saw him leaning relaxed against a bar, clever fingers toying with a book of matches, exuding power and self-confidence and raw sexuality, and the look in his eyes that would stop strong men in their tracks and turn a woman's knees to water. She saw him standing tall astride his motorcycle, looming out of the fog, helmeted and visored like a creature of legend. And she shivered with fear. He was too rough, too raw, too strong! the vulnerable female in her protested. Such a man would overpower her! Such a man could hurt her.

But...she remembered, too, all the ways he'd touched her tonight. Tucking a napkin into the front of her blouse, gently scrubbing barbecue sauce from her cheek, softly, softly brushing her cheek with his fingers, holding her hand while they walked, bringing it impulsively to his lips. And the way he'd kissed her, so lightly at first, introducing himself and that unaccustomed intimacy so gradually, awakening her responses so subtly she'd been lost before she'd even known what was happening. Lost . . . consumed by a strange, melting fire and a sweet aching, deep, deep inside. . . . Was that what it would be like, making love with Reno?

"Don't be silly," Nancy said firmly. "And stop looking so distressed. Of course you're going to go. It could be very important for your emotional growth."

"Oh," said Jenna, laughing weakly, "so it's therapy, is that it?"

"Exactly." Beaming in a self-congratulatory way, as if she'd personally invented it, Nancy gathered up her book, reading glasses and teacup and headed for the kitchen. "Something like this is just what you need to give you back the confidence and self-esteem that Jack took away from you. This Reno obviously makes you feel good, happy. . . ."

"He makes me feel beautiful," Jenna murmured, trailing after her. "And exciting. And . . . sexy."

"About time," Nancy muttered, then abruptly turned and caught Jenna's hand. "Jen—enjoy this, but be careful, okay?"

Jenna laughed, a bit uneasily. "Make up your mind. One minute you're pushing me to go for it—"

"And I think you should. But just be careful. It could be dangerous."

"I really think he knows what he's doing, Nancy. He won't let me get hurt."

Nancy gave her an odd look and said dryly, "I'm sure he does. I assume you're referring to the motorcycle? Unfortunately, that's not the only thing he has that could hurt you."

"Oh. Well," said Jenna airily while her insides turned to warm syrup, "I'm not stupid. Of course I'll be careful. I know how to protect myself." But she wasn't entirely certain that was true; she'd never had to protect herself before. As a matter of fact, right now she wasn't entirely certain of anything.

"Believe it or not," Nancy said with a wry smile, "I wasn't really referring to *that*, either." She squeezed Jenna's hand and let go of it. "Just keep it light, okay? Have fun, but don't get in too deep. You don't need that right now."

"But that's what's so great about this," Jenna said wonderingly as they climbed the stairs together. "I'm not in love. My emotions aren't involved, so I'm not vulnerable. It's like...for the first time in two years, nobody has a claim on my heart. It's *mine*, Nancy. Do you know what that means?" She paused, earnest and breathless with the miracle of it. "For the first time in two years, I'm free!"

"Well?" Twyla asked Nate when he walked in the door, "did you get there in time to meet your girlfriend?"

"Guess he must've, comin' in this late," her husband, Tom, muttered into his beer bottle.

"Geeze," Nate complained, "you'd think I was seventeen years old." But he was grinning as he sat down at the kitchen table and helped himself to a cookie from the plate in the middle of it. He bit into the cookie before he thought, then glanced at it and put it back on the plate. The bottom was black as charcoal. Twyla made probably the worst cookies in the whole damn world, but her intentions were good. "Yeah," he said with a shrug, trying to be casual about it, "I made it in time. She was there waitin' for me."

Twyla gave Tom a look that should have frostbitten his bald spot. "I wouldn't wait that long for any man. You ask me, they ain't worth it." With that she snorted, grabbed up her pack of cigarettes and stalked out; she had her rules about smoking in the kitchen. Tom sent a whoop of laughter in her wake, then turned back to Nate.

"She's mad at me because I'm on my second round," he confided with a wink, hefting the bottle of beer. "Damn it, she cut my rations again. Told me if my belly got any bigger she was gonna have to invent a new position." He leaned way back in his chair, sort of stretching and patting his stomach, shaking with silent laughter. "I asked her what she had in mind, but she wouldn't tell me. That was just about the time you walked in."

"Sorry," Nate said. "Bad timing, I guess."

Tom laughed some more, then sighed and shook his head. "Ah, hell, she'll get over it." After a pretty good swallow of beer he squinted across the top of the bottle at Nate. "She waited for you, did she? How long?"

"I don't know what time she got there," Nate said, picking up the cookie again. It didn't look any better. "I was over an hour late."

Tom gave a soft whistle. "Must be one hell of a lady." There was a little silence. Then, "You going to see her again?"

Nate frowned at the cookie and put it back on the plate. "Yeah, I am. Tomorrow."

Tom got a surprised look on his face, the look that says, "Well, I'll be damned...no kidding?" But all he said was, "Been a while for you, hasn't it, son?"

Nate shrugged. Tom drank beer, set the bottle down, picked up a cookie and bit into it, chewed thoughtfully, washed it down with more beer and finally said, "It's time."

Nate stirred restlessly. He and his foreman had been friends for a long time, but neither one of them was big on heart-to-heart talks.

"It's time," Tom said again, apparently addressing his half-eaten cookie. "Can't go on grievin' forever over what's past. It ain't easy to let go of it, I know that, I been there. Givin' up rodeoin' was the hardest thing I ever done." There was silence, followed by some throat-clearing that sounded like a bulldozer in a gravel pit. Tom abruptly shoved back his chair. "Hey, uh, you want a beer?"

Nate shook his head and stood up. "No, I think I'll go up to the cabin for a bit. I'm kind of keyed up."

Tom chuckled. "Yeah, I know what you mean. I'm feelin' a little 'keyed up' myself." He stood up, scooped his beer bottle off the table and dropped it in the trash. "Well," he said, giving his hand-tooled belt a hitch, "I think I'll go find Twyla, see if I can get her to explain about them new positions. 'Night, son."

Nate went out into the dark, chilly night, but he didn't fire up his bike, not right away. For a few minutes he stood on the front porch, petting the dogs and looking west across the valley to where round-topped hills crested with live oaks merged with the star-studded indigo sky. Beyond those hills he knew were others just like them, sheltering other ranches nested in their valleys like sleeping sparrows, and other live oaks spreading gnarled branches low and wide over sleeping beef cattle and thoroughbred horses. Beyond that, where the hills finally flattened out into the coastal plain, were the highways, housing tracts, shopping centers and eucalyptus windbreaks pushing right up against the white sandy beaches and cold green waters of the Pacific Ocean. He sure hadn't ever dreamed he'd end up this close to the ocean. To a kid growing up in Colorado, the Pacific Ocean had seemed like the back side of the moon.

Not a bad place for a wandering country boy to put down roots, he thought, shrugging his shoulders inside his leather jacket, filling his lungs with crisp, cool air. It was pretty country, especially in the spring like this, with the hills green and the wildflowers coming out—poppies and lupine and owl's clover and fields of yellow mustard. The smells of grass and flowers drifted to him on the breeze, filling his mind with visions of Jenna....

Yeah, she did smell like this, he remembered now. He'd noticed it dancing with her, and again just a while ago. It was in her hair...cool and clean, sliding over his skin like a night breeze. She smelled like...spring, he thought, like new grass and wildflowers. She smelled like the night. And like the night, she guarded her secrets.

He realized that he still didn't know much about her, but it didn't trouble him. He figured he knew all he needed to know for the moment, and finding out the rest was something he'd take his time about and purely enjoy doing. He knew that he liked Jenna and wanted her in his bed. And he knew that she wanted him for no other reason except that she couldn't help herself. He knew it from the way she'd responded to him, so openly and eagerly in spite of her shyness, with a fire and passion that were spontaneous, totally without artifice. Thinking about it made his stomach churn and his loins ache even now.

Tomorrow, he thought. He'd see her tomorrow. He already knew where he was going to take her on his bike, and he already knew her well enough to know she'd love it there. Shoot, with that quirky imagination of hers, she was bound to. He smiled as he straddled the Harley, thinking about Jenna's face lighting up with surprise, wonder, joy, pleasure. *Tomorrow...*

He sure was "keyed up," all right; there was a fire inside him that wouldn't die down, the likes of which he hadn't felt in years. But it was a different thing from those heedless wildfires of his lusty youth, white hot, fast-burning fires that consumed quickly and died for want of fuel. He didn't want that with this woman. He didn't want to rush things. He wanted her to want him and to trust him enough to let go of her shyness. He wanted her coming to him without any lingering reservations, doubts or fears. He wanted—hell, he wasn't sure how to put a name to what it was he wanted. But he knew that with her he wanted it good. Maybe even to last awhile.

Nate started the Harley's engine and pushed off with a spurt of gravel. He rode with the wind in his hair, past white fences and live oaks and clumps of dozing cattle, following well-known paths; it wasn't the first time he'd spent a restless night at the cabin, working to ease the yearning in his soul. But it occurred to him as he guided the Harley through the moonless night that for the first time in years he wasn't thinking about the past.

* * *

The noontime sky was blue, the sunshine bright enough to make Jenna wish she'd worn sunglasses, though a few wisps of last night's fog still lingered in the air like traces of perfume in the wake of a passerby, pricking the senses to vague recognition, evoking formless and disturbing memories. The memories filled Jenna's mind as she watched Reno ride toward her on his motorcycle, and though she stood tall and still, there was a curious lifting inside her. He's like a being from another world, she thought, gulping the astringent sea air as if it were an antidote. Am I crazy to be here and so happy to see him?

He wasn't wearing his helmet today, or his jacket, either, just a black shirt without sleeves and worn, faded jeans. The wind raked at his hair while the sun struck golden lights into it, so that it seemed to flicker and leap around his head like flame. As he drew nearer, Jenna could see the tattoo on his shoulder, the smooth, rounded biceps burned red-brown by sun and wind, the corded strength of forearms and wrists, hands with bone-hard knuckles and long, supple fingers. She stared at his hands, remembering the way they'd felt on her face, her neck and on the place where the swell of her breasts began....

Reno brought his bike to the curb beside her and turned off the motor. Jenna's gaze hurriedly retraced its path, from those big, capable hands on the handlebar grips, on up past muscle and sinew and tattoo, to find a slow, sweet smile spreading across his face.

"Hello, Gingerbread Lady."

It was a throaty growl, that spine-tingling purr that always produced conflicting harmonics in her. Resisting an urge to wipe her damp palms on the front of her slacks, she drew a careful breath and said, "Hi."

Reno's eyes swept over her, down to the toes of her white tennis shoes, then back up over the tan gabardine slacks to her crisp, white cotton shirt. His eyes had a black, diamond gleam. Without a word, he turned, unhooked his helmet from the seat behind him and held it out to her.

"Oh," Jenna muttered. "Thanks." She took the helmet and hefted it, staring down at it, running her hands over its smooth surface. She could feel Reno's eyes tugging at her, but she couldn't look up, not yet. She didn't want him to know that she was still quivering inside.

She'd forgotten that his eyes missed nothing. His chuckle was almost tender. "Come 'ere, darlin'," he said as he took her arm and guided her alongside the motorcycle. "Let me see that thing." He lifted the helmet from her inert hands and pulled it over her head as confidently as he'd recently tucked a napkin into the front of her blouse, as deftly as he'd wiped sauce smudges from her cheek. His hands were as warm and steady as she remembered.

"Okay now. Put your foot right here...careful of the pipes, don't burn yourself...ready?" She nodded, then gulped as his hand tightened on her forearm, just below the elbow. "Up you go...there, now. How's that feel?"

Jenna couldn't answer. She sat there frozen, awed and dumbstruck as a baby plunked into a swing for the very first time. Again, Reno's chuckle was gentle with understanding.

"You can hang on to this strap here," he said, "or you can hang on to me. First time out, you'll probably feel better holdin' on to me." He turned his head so that she could see the deepening creases at the corner of his eye, the upward curve of his lips. "I know I sure as hell will."

After a moment's hesitation, Jenna put her hands on his belt—then quickly moved them higher on his sides. In the space of a heartbeat, the heat of his body had soaked through the fabric of his shirt into the palms of her hands. Several more heartbeats passed, loud as thunder.

"Come on, darlin'," Reno drawled, not even trying to hide his amusement, "you can hold on tight, I'm not gonna break."

Her hands crept around his body. His muscles were taut as bowstrings. She felt his belly moving in and out with his breathing, felt his ribs expand and buck with his laughter.

"That's the way, now you're gettin' it. Okay, you all set?"

Jenna's head jerked up and down. She closed her eyes. "All set."

"Jenna..."

"What?" Her voice was a breathless whisper.

"Loosen up a little bit, darlin', you're stiff as a post."

Jenna opened her eyes. Reno's profile was scant inches away, chin lifted, eyes half-closed, lips curved in a half smile. He looked commanding...confident. "Oh," she said. Something—his nearness—was playing havoc with her breathing. She emitted a small, nervous sound, like a hiccup. "I'm sorry."

"It's okay," he said in the voice that reminded her of wool, soft...warm...scratchy. "Just relax a little bit. You're doin' fine."

Relax. He'd said the same thing to her, she remembered, while they were dancing.

"It's a little bit like dancing," Reno said, as if he'd thought of that, too. "You've just got to relax, go with me, don't fight me." His voice was so low she felt it in her hands, in her arms, resonating from deep in his chest. It was an interesting sensation. "Pretend you're part of me, you understand? Pretend we're one body. You go where I go, you move when I move...forget everything else. The more you relax, the easier it is for me, and the more you let go, the better it is for both of us." His smile broadened; his chest expanded, pushing against the circle of her arms. "Just like makin' love, you know?"

Oh yes. *Something* in her knew. Her body was suddenly too hot, and parts of her—her breasts and the soft place between her thighs—felt full and swollen. Her nipples tingled. She felt an intense yearning, so powerful it was almost pain, to press them against Reno's hard-muscled back, to move so close to him that the outsides of his thighs would rub all along the insides of hers and the rough seams of his jeans would press hard, hard, against the throbbing center of her body.

Her hands flexed, then flattened against his ribs. She drew a long, shuddering breath and nodded.

"Okay," Reno growled, "let's go." His muscles tensed and bucked; the Harley snarled.

To Jenna the first moments were like going over the crest of the summit on a roller coaster—a terrifying swoop that stopped her heart and blanked her mind and left her stomach behind, a dizzying plunge that tore the wind from her lungs, leaving her no breath even to scream. But when those moments had passed and she discovered that her stomach was where it belonged and her lungs were working and her heart beating again, something wonderful happened. It began with a small explosion inside her, like the popping of the cork in a bottle of champagne. Air burst from her chest in a startled rush. She felt herself expanding, swelling, filling up with glorious exhilaration. This was *fun*! It was *great*! And she thought, Why haven't I ever done this before?

They reached the end of the street. Reno leaned into the turn, and Jenna leaned with him. It gave her a giddy, weightless feeling, as if she were flying. They cornered again and she laughed out loud. And then they were racing along with sand dunes on one side and towering eucalyptus groves on the other, with the sun burning their shoulders and the jealous wind tugging at their clothes. This is freedom, Jenna thought. I'm awake, I'm alive and I'm free!

The wind-whipped ends of Reno's hair licked at the visor of her helmet. Oh, how she wanted to tear it off and feel the wind in *her* hair and his hair in her face! Laughing, she shifted her arms to hold him more tightly and felt his body shake with laughter of his own. The Harley's engine thrummed, the tires sang on the pavement and the wind whistled past her ears. To Jenna it seemed as if the whole world were suddenly new and filled with wild and glorious music.

Seven

"Why are we stopping?"

Nate answered Jenna's breathless question with a chuckle. "Because we're here."

"Oh," she said, but didn't sound as if her question had been answered. Nate could feel the movements of her body as she looked around, a complete three-sixty. Nothing but sand dunes as far as the eye could see.

Even though they'd stopped and he'd already turned off the engine, her hands were pressing so hard against his ribs it was all he could do to breathe. Not that he minded. She was still leaning against him, as much as the helmet would let her, and he could feel her body's warmth and the trip-hammer beat of her heart against his back. No, he didn't mind; he was happy to let her stay right where she was, for as long as she wanted to be there.

But . . . she was relaxing her death grip and easing away from him, so he rocked the bike onto its stand and slipped out of the saddle. When he turned around, Jenna was just taking the helmet off, shaking her head and raking through her hair with her fingers. She looked good enough to eat. Her eyes were sparkling and dancing like sunlit water, and there was color in her cheeks that made her look fresh and vivid as a bouquet of spring flowers. He saw that she had freckles, a wholesome and liberal dusting of them, and wondered why he'd never noticed them before. And then he realized that it was the first time he'd ever seen her in broad daylight.

He relieved her of the headgear and hung it up, then put his hands on her waist. "Here you go," he grunted, "watch the pipes, now."

As he lifted her off the bike and set her feet on the pavement, he thought about pulling her on in, wrapping his arms around her and kissing that sweet little mouth of hers until they both ran out of breath. That was all it took, just that thought, to kindle the fire in his belly. His eyes were drawn to the movement of her chest, much more rapid than it should have been, rising and falling under that crisp white blouse with its modest, unrevealing V. He wanted to lower his head and put his mouth there, then follow his fingers as they undid the buttons, down, down.... Her skin was hot under that blouse; he could feel the heat soaking through into his hands. Her breasts would be swollen and tight, the nipples hard, chafing against the cloth. The urge to have them in his mouth was as intense as a toothache.

But he was already so hungry for her he was about to explode, and not much had changed since last night when he'd laid out his own personal set of ground rules for this particular game. Since it wouldn't do either of them any good right now if he started something he wasn't going to finish, he peeled his hands off her sides and stepped away from her.

"Where are we?" Jenna asked, doing another three-sixty now that she was on terra firma and not seeing any more than she had the first time. She didn't sound uneasy, though. Just curious.

"There's a beach over there, the other side of those dunes," Nate said, jerking his head in that direction. He was busy unzipping the medium-sized leather carrying case he'd had attached to the back of the passenger seat; Harley-Davidsons don't come equipped with saddle bags. He handed Jenna her purse, wondered briefly why she needed such a big one, then began taking out the things he'd brought with him. "I thought we'd eat here."

"Eat? Here?"

"Yeah—kind of a picnic." Nate frowned at the two foil-wrapped packages he was holding, weighed them thoughtfully, then handed her one. "Here, I think this one's yours." He'd told Twyla to make one of the sandwiches chicken, since Jenna wasn't too sold on red meat, but he'd forgotten to tell her to mark which one was which. At least they didn't appear to be too badly squashed. "That okay with you?" he asked as he tucked a rolled up beach towel and a good-sized thermos under his arm.

Jenna was looking at him like she wasn't sure what planet he'd come from. Shoot, he thought disgustedly, to her a picnic probably meant a little red-checked tablecloth and a wicker basket full of gourmet goodies and wine in glasses. He remembered a girl in Atlanta fixing him up like that once, during a long weekend series. That was before he'd figured out that, as the song said, with the wrong person a picnic was just a cold lonely lunch on the lawn.

A smile suddenly broke over Jenna's face, like a burst of pure sunshine. "Yes," she said, "of course, it's all right. It's . . . just fine."

"Okay," Nate growled, giving her a sweeping and slightly sardonic after-you gesture. "Right this way."

It was hard work, slogging up and over those dunes, but Jenna didn't say a word. Nate went ahead so he could give her a hand when the going got rough, but when they got within sight of the water, he dropped back. He didn't want anything to interfere with her view.

"This is really incredible," she said after a while, panting a little. "It's like the Sahara. A person could almost get lost."

"Yeah," Nate said, "I guess you could." But he was smiling. Because she hadn't told him he was crazy, that they could just as well have gone to a beach that didn't take a camel caravan to get to the water.

They topped the last dune and stood there for a few minutes, looking across the last sweep of sand to where the Pacific lay sparkling in the early springtime sun. It was very quiet—no sunbathers sizzling on beach towels, no joggers pacing along the waterline, throwing driftwood sticks into the surf for their dogs' amusement, no sea gulls screeching and fighting over their refuse. But for one solitary pelican skimming the water beyond the breakers, they were alone.

"What in the world...?" Jenna said suddenly. All up and down the beach as far as the eye could see, the sand was littered with chunks of plaster, like bleached bones. She bent to pick up a piece. "This looks like—" she held it out to him for confirmation "—part of a statue!"

"Yep," Nate casually agreed, "it sure does."

"And this—" She dropped to her knees beside a larger chunk of plaster that was half buried in the sand. "This looks like...a column of some kind. Reno—" Her wide, puzzled eyes turned to him like searchlights. "What *is* this stuff? Why is it all broken and scattered? What happened here?"

"They shot a movie here," Nate said. "A long time ago—back in the twenties. One of those big Biblical epics, cast of thousands. All this—" he swung the thermos in a wide arc "—was supposed to be ancient Egypt. They built huge, elaborate sets—temples, Pharaoh's palace, a whole city, I guess—and when they were through, they left it all behind."

"Egypt..." Jenna breathed, looking fascinated then sad as she turned a plaster fragment over and over in her hands. "And this is all that's left?"

"Well, I don't know about that," Nate said, grinning because her reaction was all he'd hoped for. "There are people who think most of it is still pretty much intact."

"Really?" she cried, excited as a kid at an amusement park. "Where?"

"Could be right where we're standing." The way she was looking at him, with her lips parted and her cheeks pink, made his own heart beat faster. "Some people claim that when they were finished shooting they just laid the walls down and bulldozed 'em over with sand, and that they're still here...somewhere. Every once in a while somebody tries to get an expedition together to excavate some of these larger dunes. My personal choice would be this one, or that one over there." He pointed to a small mountain of sand farther down the beach.

Jenna shaded her eyes with her hand and gazed at it for a moment, then asked, "Why haven't they?"

Nate shrugged. "I don't know. Probably because it might be a waste of money. Most people say there's nothing buried, that it's all been uncovered and broken up long ago by wind and storms, and that what you see is all that's left. The beaches have been wearing away for years, you know." He stopped there and looked away across the rubble-strewn sand to the ocean, sparkling in the sun.

After a moment Jenna said, "But you don't think so, do you?"

"I don't know." He shrugged again, then looked at her. "But either way, I'd just as soon they left it buried."

"Yes," she said softly, "it's better like this." Her eyes were looking past him, far, far away, and he knew she was seeing it the way he always did. Not Hollywood plaster and lath, but the real thing, sandstone and terra cotta and bricks made of mud and straw, with the smells of dust and rich brown Nile mud and the babble of a thousand voices rising like heat waves into a cobalt-blue sky. *Egypt...*

A seabird called, bringing them both back with its lonely cry to the cool, pungent breeze, the damp, salty smell of the Pacific Ocean. Nate cleared his throat and shook out the beach towel. Jenna murmured "Thanks," as she sat gingerly on one end of it.

"Good a place as any," Nate muttered, joining her, careful not to crowd her. He unwrapped his sandwich and had about half of it eaten before he figured out it was the chicken he'd meant for Jenna.

The sun was high and beginning to burn through his black shirt like a branding iron. So he took it off. He hadn't planned it, it just seemed a natural thing to do at the beach, something he'd done a thousand times before in front of all sorts of people, including beautiful women. But as soon as he'd peeled the shirt off and dropped it onto the sand, sooner than the sea breeze could cool the sweat on his chest, he knew that this was something else. This was Jenna.

He saw her glance at him, open her mouth and shut it again in that way she had, as if she had something to say but lost her nerve. But she didn't look away. God, no. Her eyes slid over him like fingers, over his biceps, shoulders, chest and belly, exploring the contours of his body, testing the resilience of muscle, measuring the depth and texture of his hair. Her glance burned hotter than the sun.

"Coffee?" he asked hoarsely, holding up the thermos.

"Yes, please," she whispered.

God help us, he thought as he handed her the plastic cup to hold while he unscrewed the lid and poured. I must have been out of my mind to bring her here. I don't have enough willpower for this.

"You're left-handed," she said huskily, sounding surprised.

"Yeah." He watched her eyes travel slowly up his left arm to his elbow...concentrated on not spilling hot coffee on her hand, on carefully putting the lid back on the bottle. But when he looked back at her face he knew she'd spotted the scars.

They weren't much—modern sports surgery doesn't leave big, ugly scars—so she hadn't noticed them before. But here in the bright sunlight, and the way she'd been examining him, as if there wasn't a square inch of him she wanted to leave untouched... Hell, he thought, how was he going to explain?

For a while he thought he wouldn't have to. She sipped the hot, black coffee, not saying anything, just looking at the scars while a frown etched lines between her eyebrows. But then she passed him the cup—a spontaneous act of intimacy that both surprised and pleased him—and asked in that point-blank way she had of dealing with things that embarrassed her, "What happened to your arm?"

"Hurt it," Nate grunted, drinking coffee.

"How?"

He forced a laugh and said, "Not on the motorcycle, if that's what you're thinking." Then he surprised himself. "I hurt it," he said, "trying to make it do something the human arm was never meant to do."

"What's that?" Her voice was hushed.

His was wry. "Throw an object—a ball—as near to a hundred miles an hour as I could get it." Actually, it was the curve ball that had done him in, but that was as close to the truth as he could come without having to explain it all. "Tore some things loose. The scars are from the surgery it took to put it back together."

"Oh." Jenna nodded, then frowned. "Is it all right now? It sounds very serious."

"Nah," Nate said, "it's not serious." But he remembered the day the doctors had told him what he'd done and what it meant. *We're sorry, Nate....* They'd talked to him about odds and statistics while he'd sat there with bile burning the back of his throat, a taste he still remembered though he'd forgotten the numbers long ago. The acid taste of anger, the brassy tang of fear, the bitterness of the grief he couldn't show.

He swallowed down coffee in a gulp, handed the cup to Jenna and stood up. "Works fine," he shot back at her, bright and glib, bending down to scoop up some stones. And to prove it was, and to work off the emotional pressure building up inside him, he threw one with a sidearm snap and watched with grim satisfaction as it skipped across the water—once, twice, three times—before it sank. He followed that with another and then another, and when he could finally trust himself to look at Jenna again he found her staring at him in openmouthed wonder.

Well, shoot, it wasn't that he'd never had anybody look at him that way before. But they'd mostly been male and about ten years old. It sure hadn't ever affected him like this. Warmth filled him, driving away the cold, sick feeling in his stomach. He felt young—sort of like a ten-year-old kid himself. Grinning, full of himself as a peacock, he said, "Darlin', didn't you ever see anybody skip stones before?"

She shook her head slowly, as if entranced. So Nate scooped up another handful of pebbles and sent them skipping across the waves, one after the other, just for her. The last and largest one he hefted experimentally, and then, not really sure why, instead of sidearming it into the waves, he went into a full windup and took aim at a plaster column about sixty feet away.

Maybe it had been there all the time in the back of his mind; maybe he'd been mentally measuring the target— right size, right distance.... He sure hadn't forgotten the moves. Funny, the way it just naturally came back to him after so many years—like making love or riding a bicycle. But while his body knew what it had to do, somehow it wasn't quite right and it didn't come out quite right, either. Kind of like the way he was with music: he knew the words and he could hear the melody in his head the way it was supposed to be, but when he tried to sing, it was always just a little bit off key.

The rock sailed six feet over the column and landed with a dismal plop in the sand.

Disgusted with the effort, disgusted with himself for making it, Nate turned and walked back to the towel. He should have known better, he thought. He'd been crazy to try it.

Jenna was on her knees, digging frantically through that big purse of hers. "Wait!" she cried, breathless and pink-cheeked as if she were the one who'd just made a damn fool of herself, not him. "Oh—please. Could you do that again?" She held up the thing she'd been searching for—a thick, white drawing pad. And a pencil. Her eyes were shining like blue water. "Do you mind? Just a few more times."

What the hell? Nate thought. The lady was full of surprises. "No," he said, "I don't mind."

Again, it wasn't that he'd never done it before. He'd thrown for the world's press more times than he could remember, and an artist once or twice, too, for team promotions or whatever. He might even have thrown for a woman a time or two. But it hadn't been like this. He felt self-conscious. Nervous. As if chucking rocks at a piece of plaster was the most important thing he'd ever done or would ever do again.

So he started concentrating on what he was doing, on getting his body warm and loose, on tuning his delivery, on putting that rock where he wanted it. By the time he'd had enough, he'd worked up a sweat and he knew he was going to pay for it tomorrow, but he was hitting that damn chunk of plaster more times than not.

"Okay, that's enough," he panted, dropping onto the sand beside Jenna, who was still scratching away on her drawing pad, intent as a child. He watched her for a minute or two, letting the exhilaration in him die down, noticing the way her teeth clamped down on her lower lip, the way the sea breezes played with her hair, the absentminded way she'd reach up and tuck those teasing strands behind her ear, as easily and naturally as if she were alone. He knew she was as aware of him as he was of her, but at the same time he had a feeling she'd gone into some special place of her own and that she was letting him see a part of her she didn't let everyone see. There was a strange kind of intimacy about it. Almost, he thought, as if she were letting him watch her undress.

After a while, overcoming curious reluctance to disturb her, he coughed and said, "Well, darlin', are you going to let me see it?"

She looked startled, then hesitant. Nate saw wariness in her eyes, the same look he'd seen there when she'd told him her name. It was a look he understood. *How much of myself should I reveal to this stranger?*

It surprised him to realize how much he wanted to erase that look from Jenna's eyes, at least when she looked at him.

Finally, and without saying a word, she turned the tablet around and handed it to him. Nate took it, and for a long time he didn't say anything, either. But his heart began to beat faster and his scalp prickled with the strange electricity that was running through him. He looked up at Jenna, squinting against the sun, and asked quietly, "You do this for a living?"

She drew a quick breath and shook her head, making him think of a kid with one hand in the cookie jar. Then she looked him right straight in the eye and said, "No."

Well, Jenna told herself, it wasn't really a lie. She was a painter. She'd never been much good at graphics. But she'd been so captivated by the beauty of Reno's body, fascinated by its flawed symmetry....

Not, of course, that the male body held any particular mystery for her—she'd been working from live models since she was twelve. But she'd never seen one that affected her like Reno's did. From the first moment when she'd seen him without his shirt, she'd wanted to paint him, draw him, capture him somehow, as if by doing so she could have him forever, the way she'd tried as a child to capture sunbeams in her hands. Now, looking at the drawings she'd made, she knew that this attempt was every bit as futile.

She wanted to cry out in frustration. Her talent wasn't great enough! Pencil and paper, even paint and canvas— they were the wrong mediums. She couldn't capture the rhythm and power, the sheer poetry of his body in motion, the warmth of his skin, the heat and energy coursing beneath it. She needed more. She needed . . . something.

Maybe sculpture, she thought, looking avidly, almost greedily at Reno's hands, measuring their size and strength against her own. She'd never tried sculpture before, but now that she thought about it, from the very first moments in

Reno's arms she'd been obsessed by the feel of him, overwhelmed by the desire to *touch*. Wherever her eyes wandered, it seemed, her fingers itched to follow. The taut cords of his neck, the rounds of his shoulders, the broad planes of his chest, sweat-slicked and shiny....

A silvery drop of moisture began a slow, meandering journey across one glistening pectoral mound. She watched it, licking her lips, the desire to touch like a clenched fist in her belly, and she reached out, unthinking. Then stopped, breath catching in her throat, and lifted her eyes to Reno's face.

His smile was wry and, she thought, a little sad, as if he knew very well that she'd lied to him about the drawing. But his eyes, his all-seeing, all-knowing eyes, seemed to glow in this light, golden and warm as brandy...as if he knew very well what she wanted.

"Go ahead, darlin'," he said, that deep, deep resonance rippling across her skin like caressing fingers. "Touch me."

She was hungry for touching...starved for it. Her fingers trembled a little at the first exquisite contact, at the unexpected coolness of evaporating moisture, then flattened and spread wide, bringing her palm against firm, vibrant muscle. Her gaze followed her fingers as they smoothed beads of sweat like oil across his heated skin, and she revelled in the slipperiness of it, admiring the silken sheen, imagining the salty tang of it on her lips and tongue... The *taste* of him? Where had such a thought come from? But, oh, yes, she wanted to touch him that way, too.

She swallowed reflexively as she watched her own hand, small, blunt-fingered, slightly freckled, splayed over Reno's smooth tanned skin, her fingertips tunneling through coarse, tawny hair, her palm nesting one hard-pebbled masculine nipple. She swallowed, because the desire to put her mouth over that nipple and explore the alien textures of it with her tongue was like a powerful thirst. And because she knew that this desire, this touching, had nothing whatsoever to do with art. Her lips burned. There was a fever in her skin. She wanted to touch him with her hands, her mouth and every other part of her, to breathe in the warm, musky scent of him and absorb his heat and sweat and man smell into her very pores.

This earthiness was new to Jenna. It should have shocked her, but it didn't. It stirred and excited her, filled her with a strange, fierce exultation. She knew she was hungry for touching because it was something that Jack Remington had steadfastly denied her, but never in her wildest fantasies would she have imagined touching Jack like this. It was hard to picture him without his immaculate clothes, faultless grooming and languid elegance. Panting and sweaty—never. He'd held her at arm's length for so long, she realized now, that she'd stopped thinking of him as a real, flesh-and-blood man. He'd become an unattainable ideal to her, like a prince in a fairy tale. Jack had been a fantasy. But Reno...

The revelation, when it came, was like a burst of sunlight after a long dark night. Reno and everything that had happened to her since meeting him had seemed like a dream to her, but she suddenly knew that it was *Jack* who had been the dream. *This* was real, and perhaps for the first time in her life, Jenna was completely awake. Reno was real, beyond any shadow of doubt; she could feel his heart pounding against the palm of her hand, his vitality coursing beneath her fingers. And beyond any shadow of doubt, she knew that she wanted him.

This wanting, this fever—she didn't know what to do about it! She was certain that Reno knew and that he was waiting for a signal of some kind from her. But once she gave it, there would be no going back—she'd be on a runaway train going someplace she'd never been before. She was frightened; she wanted him and it scared her. Maybe, she thought, I'm already on that runaway train. I'm not sure I'm in control anymore.

"Reno..." She looked up at him, wordless beyond that whispered plea.

"Shh." He touched her lips with one finger, silencing her. His fingertips slowly fanned across her cheek and jaw while his thumb stroked back and forth over her lower lip, making it swell and tingle. And all the while he watched her with a gently curved smile and half-closed eyes, as if he were trying to memorize her face.

Sorcerer's eyes, she thought. Sorcerer's hands. She felt them on her neck . . . her throat . . . an almost liquid warmth flowing down the middle of her body, impeded only momentarily by the fastenings on her shirt. Deft, clever fingers dealt with the buttons the way a magician manipulates coins.

Her breath caught and then was suspended; her mouth opened. Again, Reno whispered, "Shh," although she hadn't spoken. She curled her hand unthinkingly on his chest, grazing his skin with her nails. If he noticed, he didn't mind.

His hands separated the two halves of her shirt and slowly drew them aside. Cool sea air caressed her skin, an unexpected sensation. She held very still, scarcely breathing, and felt her breasts tighten and her nipples harden and cringe away from the harshness of fabric. She felt a hush surround her, the world grow smaller. Her entire world was reflected in Reno's glowing eyes and encompassed in Reno's hands.

Is this me? she thought. Am I still Jenna? She felt most unlike herself, frozen outside, a seething cauldron within, sitting breathless and compliant in the open air while a man she barely knew undressed her. But if she wasn't herself, then why did this Jenna feel so familiar and so right? As if, she thought, it was who she was meant to be all along.

The breeze gusted, lifting her hair away from her neck, tugging at her shirt as if impatient with the pace Reno was setting. And as if suddenly impatient himself, he pushed the two halves of the shirt over her shoulders and, in the same swift motion, hooked his thumbs under her bra straps and drew them over, as well. He pulled them down to the bend of her elbows, then slipped his fingers under the lacy nylon edge and moved them inward, gently easy the material over the taut swell of her breasts.

The rasp of nylon across her tight, tender nipples made her gasp. Reno's eyes flickered upward to her face, then back down again. Jenna drew a shaken breath and closed her eyes as her breasts were laid bare to the sun and the wind, and to Reno's eyes and hands. Nothing—*nothing* had ever felt so wonderful. It was like the sense of freedom she'd experienced on the motorcycle, only more intense. The joy inside her was like pain.

She lifted her hands, meaning to help him with the fastening of her bra, but he misunderstood the gesture and held his hands out at her sides, preventing her.

"No," he said in a rasping whisper, "let me look at you."

He wished he could find a way to tell her how beautiful she was and how much pleasure he found in her. But everything he thought of to say seemed sappy to him and too much like things he'd said before. So instead of saying anything, he leaned over and kissed her. Her breath poured over his lips, bathing them with her warmth and essence; her mouth moved under his, exploring shape and texture, learning from him and teaching him, too. When he teased her lips with his tongue, she copied him, tickling him so that he exploded with soft laughter and had to stop and lean his forehead against hers for a moment.

"Open your mouth," he whispered when the laughter had died.

She complied, though the corners were still lifted with the shape of her smile. Slowly, then, he began to bathe her mouth with his tongue, the outside of her lips first, then the soft insides, the sensitive inside of her cheeks, her vibrant, quivering tongue. He heard her breath catch, then grow rapid and shallow and finally dissolve into tiny, desperate whimpers. He felt her body arch and turn in unconscious seeking. Finally, overwhelmed, she tried to turn her mouth away, but he captured her face between his hands and held her, stroking her cheeks with his thumbs while he covered her mouth and plunged his tongue deep, deep inside her. He held her until she stopped fighting it and rose up to meet him, taking all he could give and demanding more.

Jenna didn't even know it when he bore her back and down onto the sand.

Eight

She forgot where she was and even who she was. She forgot there had ever been reasons to doubt the rightness of what she was doing. With some innate though long-dormant insight, she understood that there was only one rightness, one reality, one reason for being: to assuage the terrible hunger that burned inside her. And she understood at last that the burning was nothing so trivial nor so complex as *wanting*. What she felt was a need as simple and fundamental as the need for food, and she knew with the same primal instinct that it was Reno she needed.

His strength didn't frighten her now, she reveled in it. With a wisdom as new as birth and as old as life, she knew that what she wanted was Reno's body filling the empty, aching places inside her. She wanted his hands rough, his mouth hot and savage, his weight pressing her down... down. But though she wanted mastery and dominance, there would be no sweet, sighing surrender. From somewhere in the deepest recesses of her consciousness, from the primitive jungles of her soul, something fierce and wild had been unleashed. She felt like a tigress—intensely female, strong and free. She wanted to wrap her arms and legs around Reno's powerful body, dig her fingers into his broad shoulders and score his back with her nails.

Oh, how she wanted to *touch* him! Her hands tingled and burned with the desire, almost driving her mad—but she couldn't free her arms. When Reno finally sensed her struggles and lifted his mouth from hers, her chest was heaving with frustrated passion, her breath coming in sobs.

"What is it?" he asked raggedly. "What's wrong, darlin'?"

"I want to touch you," she gasped, "but I *can't*."

Not understanding, he only chuckled softly and lowered his mouth to her swollen lips again.

But it was a different kind of kiss this time—slow and deep, drugging rather than inflaming. Her body grew heavy and liquid; she stopped trying to free her arms, and this time when Reno drew away to look at her, she gazed back at him through a sultry mist, silent and quiescent.

Smiling a slow, sweet smile, he lowered his head, brushed her mouth slightly and then shifted downward, sliding his open mouth along the edge of her jaw...its soft undercurve...the smooth, warm column of her neck. With a whispered sigh she tilted her head back, turning to give him access to the most vulnerable and vital places, the places where her lifeblood rushed and throbbed just beneath the skin. When he pressed his mouth there, her pulse filled her head with thunder, like a thousand Niagaras. She gasped, frightened by the sensation, and instantly felt the pressure ease. Reno's head moved; his teeth raked her gently. She felt the slow, erotic laving of his tongue...his lips moving along the cords of her neck in teasing nibbles. Shocked, overstimulated nerves sent cascades of shivers through her body, prickling her skin like stinging rain.

"Reno," she gasped, twisting beneath him. But she couldn't tell him, not yet.

"Easy..." His voice soothed as his hands gentled her, lightly touching her face, her neck, stroking her shoulders and arms, fanning out warm and strong over her ribs. His hands felt so good . . . so good. She arched her back, chuckling a little with pleasure when he finally slid his hands upward to cover her breasts. And when his fingers found her nipples, sensation all but swamped her. It was too much . . . *too much*. And still he went on stroking and kneading her, remolding her breasts with his marvelous hands, reshaping them, it seemed to her, changing them from virgin soft to passion heavy with just his touch. His magician's touch. . . .

Her nipples were hard . . . so hard and tight, so sensitive the breeze was too harsh a caress. *His* caress—the feathery brush of his fingertips, the butterfly flick of his tongue—was a silvery sharpness that pierced her to the core. Too much! her mind protested, even as her body writhed and shuddered, craving more.

"I want—" she panted. But Reno's hands were already under her, spreading wide across her ribs and shoulderblades as he lifted her. His mouth skimmed hot and open over her heaving breasts and closed on one eager crest.

Her breath rushed from her in a sharp, uncontrollable gasp. Reno ignored it. His mouth tugged fiercely at her, sucking hard, pulling deep . . . and deeper still. Heat and pressure pumped through her body to pool in its lowest part, and she clamped her thighs together, instinctively protective of the throbbing, aching place between them. Her hands clutched and opened in a fruitless search for something to hold on to; her head dropped back, and she moaned. *"Please . . ."*

With a heroic surge of self-control, Nate tore his mouth from her breast and with a trail of soft, quick kisses, found his way back along the bared arch of her throat to her mouth . . . and to a measure of sanity. He kissed her, their hot breaths swirling briefly together, glazed and quivering lips mumbling their inarticulate whimpers and whispered assurances, then slid his hand to the back of her head and raised her up, bringing her face into the hollow of his neck. At the same time, finally realizing that the clothing wrapped around her arms was driving her mad, he tugged it down and pushed it away.

Instantly, she lifted her hand to his neck and clung to it with a kind of desperation, fingers digging into rigid muscles, pushing restlessly through the damp feathers of his hair.

With her lips touching his neck, her warm breath flowing over his skin like fragrant oil, she whispered, "Reno...I want you to make love to me."

He sighed, "I know..." and tightened his arms around her, tightening his willpower against the feel of her breasts softly nestling in his chest hair. "I know, darlin'. And I will. I'm going to. But not here, not now." He could feel her trembling, and he began to stroke her hair, pulling it back away from her hot cheek and fingering it behind her ear. He coughed and said, "I think we ought to find a better place for it, don't you?"

She was silent, but he could feel the struggle in her, the small convulsion of her swallow several times repeated, the tickle of her lashes on his neck as she blinked. Her hand slipped from around his neck and made a white-knuckled fist squarely in the middle of his chest.

"Then why," she whispered, each word a sacrifice, "did you—did we...do this?"

"I don't know," he said truthfully, laughing a little. "Because it felt good, I guess."

She gave a small, disbelieving snort, straightened and pulled away from him slowly, looking at him like he was crazy. "Because it...*felt* good?"

"Yeah," he murmured, rubbing his thumbs across the deepening pink in her cheeks, tenderness coming unexpectedly to tighten his throat and roughen his voice. "Didn't it?"

"Well," she said, then made a prim, throat-clearing sound. "I don't think that's quite the word I'd use." Her free arm made a slender and modest V across her nakedness. She looked away.

Nate chuckled. He touched her chin and turned her back to him, but she resisted, keeping her eyes stubbornly lowered. The shadows of her lashes looked like bruises. "Jenny," he whispered, "look at me, darlin'."

The unaccustomed form of her name startled her. Her eyes flew open and looked straight into his, a clear, dark wildflower-blue. His heart gave an odd bump. "Jenny..." He said it again, then leaned over and kissed her. He drew back and exhaled slowly, letting his fingers trail down over her throat and breasts, taking her arm with it, moving it gently aside. "I kissed you...held you...because I like the way you feel, the way you look, the way you taste. I like touching you, darlin', and I plan on doing it a lot, in all the ways I can think of that'll make us both feel good. Unless you don't want me touching you, in which case you'd better let me know right now."

"No." She drew a quick, shaken breath and leaned forward into his hands. "I love the way you touch me. I'm...hungry for touching. But I thought—" She closed her eyes. He saw the confusion there anyway, and the vulnerability in her soft mouth.

"What is it?" he asked, though he thought he knew.

"The way you touched me," she said, still unable to look at him. "The way you kissed me...made me feel like I was going to explode. Didn't you—I mean, I thought you..."

"Oh, *yeah*," Nate said, laughing to keep from groaning, "I do, believe me. Here—" He caught her hand, kissed the backs of her fingers, then swiftly, before she had a chance to be shy about it, carried it to the hot, hard bulge in his jeans.

Her eyes flew open, but she left her hand where he'd put it, rubbing a little, her mouth open and awed. Nate closed his eyes, and this time didn't even try to hold back his groan. She jerked her hand away as if she thought she'd hurt him, but he caught and held it there, whispering, "No, don't stop...Jenny, your hand feels so good."

"Then why—"

He laughed raggedly; it was becoming difficult to talk...or think. "Darlin', touching doesn't have to lead to something else to feel good, does it?"

She shook her head in a preoccupied way, distracted by what she was doing with her hand. Nate began to wonder how much more feeling good he could take before "something else" became an absolute necessity.

"Touching—" he gasped "—and kissing...fooling around...is a hell of a lot of fun. It would be a shame if the only time we did it was in bed. Wouldn't it?"

"Yes," she murmured, still staring down at her hand, "I guess it would." She looked thoughtful for a moment, then smiled like a sleepy cat and leaned over to press her mouth to the hollow at the base of his throat.

It caught Nate by surprise. He croaked something unintelligible and touched her hair, then roughly tangled his fingers in it as her mouth blazed a trail of kisses across his chest. "God—Jenny," he said weakly, "what are you doing?"

She looked up at him, clear-eyed and smiling. "What am I doing?" she purred. And then he saw it—that wicked blue spark in her eyes. "Just...having fun," she said, licking her lips. And she pushed him over onto the sand.

"Wake up, darlin', we're here," Reno said softly, turning his head to bump her helmet with his chin. The Harley's engine snarled and died.

Jenna straightened slowly, feeling as if she'd awakened from a dream. "I wasn't asleep."

"Yeah? Then why'd you have your eyes closed?" His smile and drawl were gently teasing. "Still scared?"

"No," Jenna said huskily, "I'm not scared. Not anymore." She'd closed her eyes because that way she'd felt almost as if she were one with Reno, and with the bike, too. As if the lithe, strong body in her arms and the powerful machine under her were a part of her. She knew that she'd never be afraid of either of them again.

"I think I've gotten sunburned," she said as she took off the helmet. She hadn't wanted to wear it at all, but Reno had insisted. She'd wanted to ride as he did, with the wind in her face and hair.

"Come 'ere, let's see." He took the helmet from her and hung it on the handlebar, then turned on the saddle, put his hands on her waist and lifted her. She gave a startled squawk, clutched at his arms and found herself sitting across his lap, like an abducted maiden on the pommel of a saddle. "Yeah," he said in his lion's purr, brushing his fingers across her cheek, "you do look a little pink."

"That's not where I meant," Jenna muttered, growing pinker.

Reno skimmed his hand lightly over her front. "You mean..." She nodded, and he responded with a chuckle and a sympathetic, "Ouch."

She leaned her forehead against his chin and giggled. "How am I going to explain this to Nancy?"

"Why do you need to?" he asked, frowning a little.

Somewhat taken aback, Jenna said, "I don't, I guess." And she suddenly realized that she didn't want to tell her best friend about today at all, not because she was ashamed of anything that had happened, but because what she'd shared with Reno was such a personal, intensely private thing. Touching... Warmth and happiness filled her. Giving in to an overwhelming desire to touch him again, she placed her hands on his face and smiled into his dark, probing eyes. "I don't have to tell her a thing."

"I take it your friend doesn't approve of me?"

"On the contrary," Jenna murmured, lightly stroking his lips with a fingertip and marveling at the satin-smoothness of them. "She's the one who told me I should go out with you."

"Hmm. Seems to me you're a big girl," Reno said mildly. "You couldn't decide that for yourself?"

"Well..." She was gazing at his mouth, flooded with memories of the way it had felt...tasted. She licked her lips. "I've been a little lacking in confidence...lately."

"Oh yeah? How 'bout now?"

She gave a smug little chuckle and closed the small distance between her mouth and his. He feigned surprise for a second or two, then made a pleased sound low in his throat and opened his mouth under hers. For another few moments he let her have things her own way, and then he arched over her, bearing her down into the cradle of his arms, and kissed her long and deep.

Neither of them wanted to end it, so it went on for quite a while...sweet, sensual meanderings through territories already grown familiar. Though not less exciting for being so. Just more carefree. Glazed lips touching smiles, tongues dipping and twining in breathless mouth play...honeyed murmurs, sultry sighs, and gusts of champagne laughter. Unnoticed and unheeded, the sun sank through a reddish haze into a purple fogbank and the evening star winked on in the lavender twilight. A car passed by on the street with its headlights on.

"I'd better go," Jenna whispered, slurring the words.

"Jenny, come home with me tonight."

Shudders of desire rippled through her. "I can't...I promised...."

He sighed and stroked her hair. They'd had this conversation before, at the beach. "I know." He eased her off of his lap and held her while she tested her legs. "You okay?"

She nodded dumbly, then shook her head. She felt...swollen. Hot. Her arms and legs felt jerky and uncoordinated. She was shaking. She said grumpily, "I feel like I've been run over by a truck."

Reno's laugh was soft and ironic. "Me, too, darlin'."

She swayed forward blindly, found his mouth unerringly. He kissed her hard, then put her from him. "Go," he growled, "before I say to hell with your friend."

It was, Jenna decided, the hardest thing she'd ever done. It wasn't like having part of her torn away, it was more as if she couldn't separate herself from him at all. As if she were still connected to him by an elastic band of some kind that stretched tighter and tighter as she moved away from him, so that she felt its tension and pull on every muscle in her body.

She unlocked her car, opened the door and turned to look back at him.

"I'll call you," he said softly.

She nodded and murmured, "Okay."

He laughed and muttered something about cold showers. The Harley's engine growled. Its headlight stabbed through the dusk.

Jenna started her car and sat for a moment before she remembered that Reno wouldn't leave until she did. The thought of his caring gave her a feeling of warmth and pleasure. "Drive carefully," she whispered, smiling into the rearview mirror.

As his headlight grew smaller and smaller behind her, she felt the elastic band grow tighter and tighter, until its pull was an ache in every part of her.

But it's just sex, she told herself. I'm not in love.

The attraction is purely physical. My heart's still free.

It's just sex.

She told herself that over and over, all the way to Nancy's, and by the time she got there, she believed it.

Cold shower, hell, Nate thought disgustedly as he watched Jenna's taillights disappear in the distance. What he needed was a fire hose.

It had to be a first for him, letting things go so far without carrying them to their natural conclusion. He wasn't sure why he'd done it. He could have taken her someplace—a motel or something. She'd wanted it as much as he had. But it was funny—in spite of the fact that he wasn't entirely sure he hadn't done himself permanent injury, he felt good about it. Damn good.

By the time he got home the ache in his loins had subsided. His arm was another story. Well hell, he thought ruefully, it was no more than he deserved. He'd been crazy to throw like that. His throwing days were over.

He parked the Harley, unzipped the carrying case and took out the thermos and the rolled-up drawing Jenna had done of him at the beach. He tucked the latter under his arm while he doled out pats and hugs to his canine welcoming committee, then clomped up the steps and let himself into the kitchen.

Twyla came shuffling out in her slippers and bathrobe while he was rinsing the thermos in the sink. She was carrying her lighter and an unlit cigarette, and had her hair rolled up in great big plastic curlers.

"Hi, hon," she croaked, "have a good time?"

Nate glanced at her. "Yeah, I did."

"Here, let me do that." She took the thermos from him and elbowed him out of her way. Nate opened the refrigerator door and peered inside. Twyla glanced at him and said, "You hungry?"

"No, I guess not." Nate slammed the refrigerator and opened the freezer instead.

"Can I get you something?" Twyla asked dryly. "Or are you just cooling off?"

"Ice," Nate said, frowning. "I need some ice."

"Well, get out of there and I'll get it. What do you want it in—ice tea? Water? Scotch?"

"No, a bowl," Nate said. "A big bowl, just a little bit of water. And a dishtowel."

He went into his office, sat down at his desk and unrolled the piece of paper. When Twyla came in a few minutes later, he was still sitting there, frowning at it.

"What's that?" she asked, stretching to see over his shoulder while she was reaching past him to put the bowl of ice on his desk. Twyla wasn't nosey; she just naturally considered Nate her business.

He turned the sketch so she could see it. She looked at it for a moment without comment, then said, "Not bad," which for Twyla was rare praise. "She an artist or something?"

Nate grunted. "Yeah, or something."

Twyla gave the drawing and his arm some pointed looks and shuffled out, leaving him to the ordeal of icing down his elbow. *Damn*, but he'd forgotten how much that stuff hurt!

Once he'd gotten the arm pretty well numbed, he picked up the drawing with his right hand, absently rubbing his thumb over the scrawled initials in the lower righthand corner.

J.M. Jenna . . . what? He'd bet his ranch it wasn't Miller.

She'd lied to him this afternoon about the drawing, and there was no use pretending to himself he didn't mind. He'd hoped maybe she'd open up with him a little more, maybe because he was starting to feel like telling her things about himself. Like he'd told her about his arm, which had surprised even him. And like he'd *almost* told her about the baseball. Damn it, it hurt that she still didn't trust him enough to let him know who she was, when she sure didn't seem to have any trouble trusting him in other ways.

Shoot, he thought, if she wasn't a professional artist, she should be. That drawing—just a pencil sketch done on the spur of the moment, but with so much power and motion in it he could smell sweat, hear his own grunts of effort, feel the stretch and pull of his muscles and tendons.

Nate pushed the paper angrily away from him and began to paw through the mess on his desk for the notepad he'd scribbled her car's license number on. All right, if that was the way she wanted it, she wouldn't tell him who she was, he knew there was somebody at the DMV who'd be glad to do Nate Wells a favor!

And then he sank back, closed his eyes and exhaled slowly through his nose. *No.* He wasn't going to do that. He wanted Jenna to let him into her life because she wanted him there. He'd just have to be patient, that was all.

"Earth to Jenna . . ."

"Hmm?" Jenna said, emerging from a somewhat confusing and extremely disturbing daydream.

Nancy shot her a quizzical look. "Jen, I just told you I was thinking about getting a moosehead to go with those slacks I bought, and you said, 'That's great, Nance.'"

"Oh," said Jenna. "Oh, God, I'm sorry, I was just... thinking."

"Hmm, no kidding. You know, Jen, not that it hasn't been fun shopping with you, but I don't know why you didn't just go with him. I think that's where your mind is anyway."

"I know," Jenna groaned. "It's terrible. I feel like such a... Here, I came to see you, and it seems like all I've done is run out on you."

"You haven't run out on me. I've had to go to work, after all. I'd have been running out on you, if you hadn't found something to occupy your time."

"Yes, but I really was looking forward to having today to spend together. I'm glad we did this. I haven't been shopping at a mall in years."

Nancy looked at her. "And all you bought was a pair of jeans? I can't believe it. My best friend is becoming a biker."

"I am not," Jenna said, half laughingly, half defensive. "I just thought, if I'm going to be riding a motorcycle, I should have something more appropriate to wear than slacks, that's all."

"Uh-huh." The tone of bald skepticism was mitigated by the glint of laughter in Nancy's eyes. After a pause she said casually, "And how was your date yesterday? You haven't said much about it."

Carefully matching her shrug and tone to Nancy's, Jenna said, "Oh, it was fun. I had a good time. We went to the beach. Reno brought some sandwiches." At least, she thought, as far as it went it wasn't a lie.

"Well," Nancy said dryly, "that explains the sunburn."

Jenna couldn't say anything. She kept her eyes steadfastly on the road ahead. It ran straight as an arrow at this point, right to the foot of the dark green hills that formed a natural bulwark against the brooding bank of coastal fog. Now that the sun had gone down, tendrils of fog were beginning to reach like fingers over the crests of the hills, a chilling effect, like something out of a horror movie. So why, Jenna wondered, did her whole body feel hot, as if she were still lying in the burning sun....

After a while, breaking what had become a curiously difficult silence, Nancy looked over at her and said, "You know, it's been my experience that when someone stops talking about a relationship, it usually means it's either going sour or going intimate. It's too soon for this one to be going sour, so..." She took a deep breath and faced forward again. "Forgive me, Jen, I have to ask you—are you sleeping with him?"

"No," Jenna said, turning to look out of the window, then added softly, "not yet."

The telephone began to ring as they were letting themselves in the back door, and since Nancy didn't have an answering machine they both ran for it, dropping packages and purses on the kitchen floor. Nancy picked it up, said, "Just a minute," and with her face carefully devoid of expression, handed it over.

"Hello, darlin'." Reno's soft, scratchy voice sent vibrations of pleasure rippling outward from Jenna's ear to all the parts of her body that remembered his touch. "Did you have a good time?"

"Yes, I did," Jenna murmured, unconsciously trying to hide her face from Nancy's all-too-perceptive gaze. "I—we had a great time." *And all I did was think about you. You knew I would, didn't you?*

His chuckle answered her unspoken question. "How 'bout tomorrow? Feel like goin' for another ride?"

"Yes, I'd like that. What time?"

"Noon. I'll pick you up—"

"You don't have to do that. I'll meet you."

There was a pause, and then a soft, ironic laugh. "All right, Gingerbread Lady. I'll see you tomorrow at Smoky Joe's."

Jenna listened to the sound of the disconnect, but for a moment or two went on holding the receiver next to her cheek, biting her lip and frowning at nothing. Something in the pause, in that soft laughter, in the tone of his voice told her she'd disappointed him. She found that thought unexpectedly discomfiting.

Nancy was at the sink, filling the teakettle. Without turning she said, "So you're seeing him again tomorrow?"

"Yes." Jenna hung up the phone and stared at it, still frowning.

"And are you going to be coming home tomorrow night?" Nancy's question was blunt, but her voice sounded curiously muffled.

Jenna turned to look at her. "I don't know," she said quietly. "But don't worry about me...if I don't." Then, taking a deep breath and folding her arms across her body in an unconsciously defensive gesture she asked, "What would you think of me if I didn't?"

Nancy put the teakettle on the stove, turned on the gas and finally looked up at her. "You mean, am I going to think you're a terrible person if you decide to sleep with a man on the...what is it, the third date? Fourth, if you count dancing with him that first night. Nowadays, I imagine that's pretty conservative, Jen." She tried to smile, then gave it up and shrugged instead. "Plus, you're almost thirty years old, you don't need permission. If it feels right to you, that's all that counts, right?"

Jenna said softly, "Yes, but I care what you think."

Drawing a deep but not-quite-steady breath, Nancy said, "Look, you're my best friend, I'm not going to sit in judgment. Even if you slept with a complete stranger, I wouldn't think you were a terrible person. But I'd sure as hell worry about you."

"You don't need to worry about me," Jenna muttered. "I know what I'm doing."

"Do you?" Nancy tossed the towel she'd been drying her hands on in the general direction of the counter. "Look, Jen, I know you. You were really in love with Jack Remington. You got hurt—badly. Now you're on the rebound—classic case. This guy—who, in case you hadn't noticed, just happens to be the antithesis of Jack—sweeps you off your feet, carries you off on his big black motorcycle.... *Please*, just remember this *isn't real*. Your heart isn't ready to fall in love yet. This has to be just a fling, something to help you feel good about yourself again. He's giving you something you really need right now, and you're responding to it. Just don't start believing it's the real thing."

Jenna cleared her throat and said carefully, "What if it is?"

Nancy snorted. "For heaven's sake, Jen."

"Well, is it so impossible?" Jenna asked with a certain belligerence. "Why *couldn't* I fall in love with Reno?"

"Be serious. You're Jenna McBride, have you forgotten? Your parents' work hangs in the Norton Simon, the New York Met, not to mention the White House! And while your career might be in hiatus at the moment, your own stuff sells for five figures in some of the ritziest galleries on two continents. You can have *anybody*. Jen, this guy may have charisma oozing out of every pore, but he's a biker, for God's sake. He has no visible means of support."

"He said he was employed." Jenna twitched her shoulders as if to shake off an unwelcome touch.

"Yeah? Doing what? He sure seems to have all the leisure time in the world to spend with you!"

"Maybe I like that," Jenna said, suddenly almost shouting. "I don't need anybody to support me. Maybe I'd *like* having someone with nothing better to do than pay attention to me!"

"Are you in love with him?" Nancy asked quietly, her blue eyes shadowed with concern. "Is that what you're saying?"

"No, of corse not," Jenna snapped. "What a ridiculous idea. I'm never going to fall in love again, it hurts too much." Fighting back tears, swallowing the ache in her throat, she bent over to pick up the packages and purse she'd dumped on the floor.

"I think he's good for me, Nancy," she said with a laugh that wasn't entirely without tears. "I even...I did some drawing yesterday. Of him. At the beach. For the first time in months, I felt like painting."

Nancy came over to put her arms around her. "Well," she said huskily, "as long as he's making you happy, Jen. That's all that counts."

Nine

Jenna slept badly and awoke several hours before dawn, clammy and sweating, besieged by a vague sense of guilt. Which wasn't surprising, perhaps, given the fact that she was about to embark on an affair for the first time in her life. But the strange thing was, in spite of the circumstances, she really couldn't account for the feeling. There just wasn't anything in her background, upbringing or personal system of values that should have made her feel guilty about going to bed with a man, with or without marriage or declaration of love. The fact that she'd never done so before had nothing to do with moral convictions. She certainly didn't consider it *wrong*. She and Reno were both responsible, single adults, and what they did together concerned no one but themselves.

So she told herself over and over again as she pounded her pillow and tried to find a cool place between the sheets for her fevered body. But at last, instead of the longed-for oblivion of sleep, she fell into a state of half consciousness in which her mind was free to wander, not quite randomly, as it does in dreams, but over the well-traveled pathways of recent memory.

She thought of Reno, which again wasn't surprising. She'd thought of very little else, these last few days. But until now she'd been aware of him mostly in terms of herself—first as her mysterious savior and then as a man whose very *differentness* fascinated and excited her. For a while, at least, she'd circled him the way a lion tamer armed only with a chair approaches a dangerous jungle cat, wary and suspicious, always trying to assess his thoughts and gauge his next move.

And then... Oh, Lord, he'd kissed her. And after that she'd been able to think of nothing at all but the way she felt when he touched her. The way her heart pounded and her chest tightened so that it was hard even to breathe. The way her body felt—so hot, burning on the outside, melting inside. And the way that even remembering his touch could make her stomach twist and her skin flush and her legs grow weak as water.

But now, in the lonely predawn darkness she was remembering Reno differently. Perhaps for the first time, she was really seeing *him*. All at once she remembered the wariness in his eyes when he'd asked her about her family, and the slightly bitter twist to his lips when she'd assured him she was single. She heard the uncertainty that sometimes crept into his voice with the seemingly casual, "If that's all right with you..." And the too-casual, almost indifferent way he'd said, "You're going to have to decide whether or not to trust me," when she knew he hadn't been indifferent at all. And other things...so many other things he'd said. The set of his mouth, the look in his eyes.

His eyes. *Merlin's eyes.* Before, she'd only noticed the way they looked at *her*, probing her heart, searching her soul. It hadn't occurred to her that those same eyes might reveal what was in his. Now she remembered the times he'd hidden them from her, lowering his lashes like curtains, or even walking away, as he'd walked away from her on the beach, after she'd asked about his scars, and picked up stones to keep her from seeing the pain in his eyes. *Pain?* Oh, she could see it clearly now. Why hadn't she noticed it then?

Maybe, she thought, because she'd been too busy looking at him to really *see* him. Studying him as an artist studies her subject, measuring the proportions of his body, admiring its grace and power and symmetry, mentally translating three-dimensional muscle and sinew into lines and shading on paper and canvas. And missing completely the small imperfections that made him a flesh-and-blood man. Those scars on his elbow... and another, smaller one on his side, just above the waistband of his jeans. The hair on his chest and the dark line of it down the center of his belly. She hadn't known how soft it would be or how much she'd like the way it felt against her own skin. She hadn't known she could made a strong man groan just by nuzzling through his hair and pressing her open mouth against his quivering belly.

She hadn't known that lying here alone in the still of night, she could bring back so vividly that primal sound, the smell of sun-warmed skin, the feel of taut muscle trembling against her tongue, that her own body would grow heavy and sultry at the memory and throb like an aching tooth....

Dawn came almost as blessed relief. Even the mockingbirds' raucous screeching, heralding the passage of the neighbor's cat out and about for his morning prowl, was a welcome distraction. As before, Jenna thought of her grandparents' house and the palm trees, the orange tomcat and the summer of Camelot. But this time it didn't make her smile. For some reason, thinking about the Camelot stories disturbed her so much that she got out of bed at that unprecedented hour and went into the bathroom and turned on the shower.

It wasn't until later, with her eyes closed tightly under a cascade of shampoo and warm water, that she realized what it was that troubled her.

Merlin. Reno reminded her of Merlin. Merlin the wizard, the all-knowing, the wise and compassionate teacher...

Oh, yes, it was true that in Camelot legends, the wizard Merlin was possessed of knowledge and understanding far ahead of his time. But, she remembered, Merlin was also a man, and vulnerable. In the end, so the story goes, he falls in love, is seduced and ultimately betrayed. By a woman.

Jenna stayed in the shower for a long time, until the room was steamy and her skin bright pink, trying to drown the cold unease that trickled down her spine.

Reno was waiting for her, sitting relaxed astride the Harley, legs spread wide, arms folded on his chest. He was wearing jeans and a white T-shirt that hid his tattoo but not his muscles. His black-visored helmet was hanging from one handlebar, but his hair looked as windblown and sunburnished as ever, which made her suspect he hadn't been wearing the helmet. Altogether, Jenna thought, he looked powerful, intensely masculine and more than a little dangerous.

She attributed the sudden upsurge she felt in her belly at the sight of him—much like what happens when an elevator stops too suddenly—to nervousness. Likewise she regarded a certain shortness of breath and the tendency of her hands to tremble when she took them from the steering wheel. Her emotions, however, were more difficult to account for. They were such a jumble, for one thing, and there were many she couldn't even identify. But the one she felt most and couldn't avoid acknowledging was *joy*. Joy—pure, warm and unmistakable as the sun. And like the sun, she could neither question its existence nor dare to look at it too closely.

She got out of the car, locked it and walked toward him, self-conscious in her stiff new jeans. Reno's eyes swept down, down the whole length of blue denim to the toes of her white tennis shoes and back up again.

"Hello, darlin'," he said as a slow, sweet smile broke over his face. "Been shopping?"

"Well," Jenna began, her skin prickling hot-cold with awareness of the way his eyes touched her like warm, brown hands, "I thought if I was going to... I didn't really have anything—"

"Hey," Reno said abruptly, interrupting her. "Come 'ere."

His tone was imperious, the little jerk of his head an implicit command. His whole attitude—eyes heavy lidded and sultry, folded arms with their macho display of biceps—was supremely self-confident. Impossibly arrogant. And, oh, what a strange and powerful effect it had on Jenna. All at once she felt self-confident, too. She felt exciting and sexy, her body lush and supple. Her walk slowed... her hips moved with a graceful, feminine rhythm.

A foot or so away from him she stopped, taunting him, one hand on her hip, her sleepy-eyed smile a reflection of his. He laughed with sheer delight, a sound as rich and intoxicating as rum. His strong hands grasped her hips; his arm muscles bulged beneath her hands. Laughter rose in her like froth as he lifted her and dragged her roughly across the saddle.

"Doesn't matter what you wear," he growled in a voice as bumpy and unreliable as a gravel road. And that was all. But Jenna, lying back against the firm support of his arm, with her hip snugly nestled in the V of his well-worn jeans, had never felt so complimented nor so beautiful. His eyes, traveling slowly from her lips to her throat, lingering on the gentle swell of her breasts, said everything he couldn't say with words.

His hands hovered over her chest, measuring its erratic rise and fall while his fingers toyed with the top button of her blouse, then swept on down and came to rest in the hollow of her stomach, just above the waistband of her jeans...a deliciously warm and vital weight. If he moved his fingers just a little, he could slip them under her waistband—clever fingers—and easily find his way past the barriers of cotton and nylon to the hot, moist flesh that craved his touch.

I wonder if he knows, she thought as she hooked her hand around his neck, tangled her fingers in his hair and lifted herself into his hungry, hot kiss. I wonder if he knows... regardless of what happens between us today, or tonight, or tomorrow, that he has already claimed and possessed me....

From somewhere nearby a door slammed. Voices, talking, laughing flared loud and then receded. A car drove by in the street, multiple stereo speakers thumping.

Reno pulled away slightly and muttered, "Let's get out of here before I do something I could get arrested for." He eased Jenna into an upright position, put both hands on her shoulders and looked deep into her eyes. "You do terrible things to me, Gingerbread Lady," he drawled, one side of his mouth tilting upward in a wry half smile. "Sometimes I think I'm the one in danger of drowning."

A silvery dart of pain pierced Jenna's heart unexpectedly. She winced and, on an impulse reached up to lay her hand on the side of Reno's face. He caught her wrist, kissed the tips of her fingers and turned suddenly, twisting his body to reach something behind him. "Ooops, almost forgot," he grunted. "Here—I brought you a present."

"A... present?" The silver shaft in her heart turned and twisted. She caught her breath as he dropped the smooth, shiny helmet into her hands.

Reno shrugged and looked endearingly uncomfortable. "Yeah, I figured I'd better get you your own headgear. This one ought to fit you better than mine does, anyway. Here, let's see. Put it on."

"I can't believe you bought me a helmet," Jenna whispered as he tugged it gently over her hair. The pain in her heart was blossoming, threatening to embarrass her. "So expensive... you didn't need to do that. Thank you...."

"Ah, hell," he growled, tilting her visor up and brushing a knuckle across her cheek, just below her eye, "I know it isn't flowers, but..." A smile creased his eyes and gave his rugged features that certain poignancy... a heart-melting sweetness. Then he laughed, dropped a quick kiss on the only part of her he could reach—her nose—and taking her firmly by the waist, lifted her down from his lap.

"Hop on, darlin', let's go." He reached for his own helmet, then suddenly paused, dropped Jenna a wink and a foxy grin and intoned, "Jump on my back, Miss Gingerbread Lady...."

Jenna laughed as she climbed onto the seat behind him and wrapped her arms around his ribs, but it was laughter that hurt. She was beginning to wish devoutly that she'd never mentioned that silly nursery tale. If ever an analogy seemed less apt...

He'd bought her a helmet. Not flowers or candy or even jewels, but something more than all of those things. More personal. More...permanent. The more Jenna thought about it, the more she couldn't ignore the significance of the gift, and the more it terrified her. A cataclysm of fear and guilt shook her.

"Hang on, darlin'," Reno shouted as he kicked the Harley off its stand, misunderstanding the shudder that rocked her.

Hang on she did, as hard as she dared, and closing her eyes, she tried to lose herself in the heat and scent of his body, the heartbeat rebounding against her breasts and hands, the powerful engine pulsing between her thighs...and in doing so, forget that she'd ever had a conscience.

Nate took them inland over little-known roads, staying away from the freeway. It was the way he liked to travel, zipping along narrow paved roads between truck farms and groves of towering eucalyptus, remnants of the forests planted in the last century by entrepreneurs hoping to get rich providing the railroads with a ready source of railroad ties. Nate loved the groves, especially after rain or on a day like today, with the sun bright and hot and an on-shore breeze blowing. Ordinarily he'd ride without a helmet just to have that cool wind in his hair and the pungent, medicinal smell in his nostrils, but he didn't want Jenna picking up his bad habits. He hadn't known her long, but he sure as hell knew he didn't want any kind of harm to come to that lady.

Much as he liked the land and the trees, though, it was the towns Nate really loved, dusty little farm towns the freeway had bypassed and the world had somehow left behind. Where old men wearing blue work shirts and a week's worth of beard stubble still sat on the porch of the hardware store and talked about the weather and baseball and what the world was coming to. Where a barefooted child walking home from the corner store with a quart of milk and a loaf of bread in a brown paper sack, gnawing on a candy bar and counting change... looked up in surprise and then smiled and waved as the big black bike roared past him.

He could have been that child, Nate thought as he waved back. He wondered if the kid was dreaming, as he had, only of someday getting out of that rural backwater town and into the big wide world, where things *happened*. And if he ever did get out, how long it would take him to find his way back.

Jenna's arms tightened impulsively around him, as if she'd been moved by some emotion that had to be shared, even though she couldn't talk to him or see his face. And he thought to himself, To hell with brooding about the past! This was the present, and the present was Jenna pressed against his back, wearing her brand-new jeans and the helmet he'd bought her, stroking him with unconscious sensuality through the fabric of his shirt. And the future? Ah, the future... Nate took a deep breath and let laughter tumble through him, loosening everything up inside him so that for the first time in years he felt carefree... happy.

They stopped to eat in Los Olivos, at a little deli Nate knew about. He ordered his usual—pastrami and chopped liver on rye, a taste he'd acquired during those long sojourns in eastern cities. Jenna looked at him like he was out of his mind and ordered turkey on whole wheat, but when Nate offered her a bite of his sandwich, she decided she liked his better. So he traded her, half for half, even though he wasn't crazy about turkey.

They sat at a table outside under an arbor and watched people—very few people—strolling up and down the street.

There would be a lot more, Nate told her, on the weekends, when art collectors from Santa Barbara and Los Angeles came up to prowl the galleries the town was known for.

"Do you like art?" he asked, keeping his tone lazy and his manner casual, trying to watch Jenna without looking like he was. "We could check out a few of the galleries, if you want to."

When he mentioned the galleries, she sort of dove into her sandwich, as if she were either starving to death or trying to hide in it. And when he asked her the question about art, her lashes came down like curtains. She chewed earnestly for several seconds and carefully patted her lips with her napkin. Then she coughed, lifted guileless blue eyes to him and said with what sounded like genuine surprise, "Art galleries?"

"Yeah, sure," Nate said. "Some of it's just tourist stuff—you know, landscapes, seascapes, big-flower watercolors—but there are good things, too. Some pretty well-known artists. If you're interested—"

"I'm not really in the mood for art galleries," she interrupted, smiling brightly to soften the edge in her voice. She glanced almost furtively at the row of buildings across the street. "The weather's so beautiful. Can't we just ride on...maybe forever?"

"Sure, darlin'," Nate drawled, smiling back at her, though some of the sunshine had gone out of his day. He told himself he couldn't force it, he knew he had to just be patient, but he couldn't help feeling disappointed. *Jenny...Jenny, when are you going to decide to trust me?* "If that's what you want. Ready to go?"

She breathed, "Oh yes," and jumped up, her relief so obvious he almost laughed. She really shouldn't ever try to lie to him, he thought sardonically; she was so damn bad at it.

But as they cleared away their paper plates and napkins and walked back to the bike, she kept glancing at him with wary and troubled eyes, as if she knew she'd hurt him and was sorry.

It's so beautiful, Jenna thought, her emotions and senses overwhelmed by the assault of colors as vivid and unlikely as a child's painting. The sky was an impossible blue, seamless and opaque as construction paper, with fat white construction paper clouds pasted on, the hills emerald green and primary yellow, the new-leafed live oaks something in between. Even the cattle looked like something a child might draw—fat, oblong boxes with little stick legs, in mottled yellow, red-brown and glossy black.

Reno brought the Harley to a halt at a stop sign and flipped on the turn signal. Jenna glanced around. Seeing nothing but fields full of grazing horses bordered by white rail fences, she tapped him on the shoulder and asked, "Where are we?"

He flipped up his visor, grinned and knocked gently on hers.

Jenna muttered, "Oops," and lifted her visor. "I was just wondering where we're going. Isn't this a private driveway?"

"Yep," Reno said, "it sure is. I thought I'd show you my place. If that's all right with you."

"Your place? You mean...you live *here*?"

He nodded. "Live and work."

"Work?" Jenna looked again at the horses, the sweeping vista of pastures and hills, almost speechless with wonder. "Are you," she finally managed to ask, "a... *cowboy*?"

He threw back his head and laughed, then said thoughtfully, still chuckling, "No, actually I think I'm probably more of a bookkeeper."

Jenna just looked at him. She wondered if it was possible he was being serious. He didn't seem completely serious, but....

"So...what about it?" Reno twisted in the saddle to look at her, his eyes like rapiers. "You want to see where I spend my time, or are you still afraid to trust me? Just say the word, darlin', and we'll go someplace else."

"No," Jenna said, "of course not. I want to see your place." Her visor snapped shut.

But not before Nate saw the fear and worry in her eyes. It amazed him how much it hurt and disappointed him to see them there.

Nobody was in sight as they sped past the main house, not even the dogs, who ordinarily came out en masse to give him a noisy welcome home. Probably all up in the north pasture with Tom and the hired hands vaccinating those calves, he thought, which was just as well. The way Jenna had talked about dogs the other night, she'd probably have wanted to stop and pet 'em all, and then chances are Twyla'd come out to see what the racket was, and he'd have to answer some questions he wasn't ready for. He wasn't sure why he didn't want Jenna to know the ranch was his, he just knew that for the time being he was enjoying having her think he was nothing but a motorcycle bum who'd be hard strapped for the cost of a new helmet.

The road to the cabin was rough, not more than a track in some places. Nate took it as easy as he knew how, but it was still a bumpy ride. Jenna never once flinched or tensed up, just rode the way he'd taught her, completely relaxed, one with him and the bike. It gave him some comfort to know that if she didn't trust him in any other way, at least she seemed to have plenty of confidence in the way he handled his Harley.

It was always a little bit of a thrill, though, to drop down into the creek wash, rumble over the wooden bridge and then go swooping up the other side at high rev. When he pulled up in front of the cabin, Jenna was shaky and breathless, like a kid getting off a roller-coaster ride.

"Oh, boy, wait a minute—my legs are still shaking," she said, laughing as she handed him her helmet. He put his hands on her waist to steady her while she dismounted, and she caught at his arms for support. "Can we go back and get my stomach? That was—" She broke off when she saw the cabin.

Nate looked at it, too, not saying anything, just waiting to see what she'd say, wondering what she thought of it. He tried to see it through a stranger's eyes and had to admit it didn't look like much, especially on the outside. He had no idea how old it was or who might have built it originally. He thought it might have been a settler's cabin or maybe a line shack for one of the early ranchos. It was built in the early-Spanish style, a low rectangle with a veranda running all along the front. The walls were a foot thick and made of adobe and rocks carried up from the creek. The floor of the veranda was adobe brick, worn down in front of the doorway from decades of foot traffic. Nate hadn't done much to the outside, except dig a septic tank and put on a new roof of fireproof shingles, but he'd spent quite a bit of time and money making the inside liveable. He'd put down a real wood floor, paneled the rough adobe walls, added on a lean-to in the back for a kitchen and bathroom, brought in a propane tank for heating and cooking. He was still thinking about whether he wanted to install a generator or not.

He unlocked the door he kept padlocked against vandals and ushered Jenna in ahead of him. He waited for her eyes to adjust to the dimness, then coughed and said, "Well, this is it. My hiding place."

He heard the long sigh of her breath. "Perfect," she whispered, almost as if she were talking to herself.

Perfect. Reno's cabin was just like him, Jenna thought—a little rough on the outside, but basically rugged and strong, with unexpected beauty inside.

She went on into the cabin's one large room, drawn by the warmth of golden wood, rich brown leather and Navaho rugs, the friendly clutter of books. There were bookcases all around the room, some filled with well-worn paperbacks, others with small pieces of sculpture done in wood and clay. There were even a few in bronze. I don't believe this, she thought, silent and wondering, overcome by all the things she was learning about Reno. He collects *sculpture*.

And then she saw the table.

It was at the far end of the cabin near a window, in the middle of a particular kind of disarray that Jenna instantly recognized. Regardless of medium, few artists are neat. The table and the floor around it were spattered with clay, littered with tools, rags, blocks of clay, pieces of wood and battered containers of various sizes and purposes. In the middle of the table was an indistinguishable mound covered with cloth.

She turned, heart hammering, skin cold and prickling with shock, and whispered, "You're...a sculptor?"

Reno laughed and came toward her, looking endearingly and uncharacteristically awkward. "Ah, hell no. I just do this for fun. Relaxes me, you know? I've always done it, ever since I was a kid. My grandpa taught me. He always used to whittle, make things with his hands, carve things out of wood...."

"These are beautiful," Jenna said, strolling from bookcase to bookcase, touching pieces here and there. One in particular, a small carved mountain lion that seemed to leap right out of the wood, she couldn't resist picking up. Wanting to experience its lifelike warmth and satiny texture, she turned it over in her hands, admiring the way the wood's own grain had been used to give an illusion of motion. "Really...beautiful."

"That's an old one," Reno said, again with that poignant awkwardness. "I must have been in high school when I made that. When I was a kid I lived in a little mountain town in Colorado, so I mostly did animals." He gave a short and curiously harsh laugh. "I guess because that's what I saw the most of."

Jenna put the lion back on its shelf and moved on. "When did you do these?" she asked, picking up a figure of a man and turning it this way and that. It gave her an impression of harnessed power, an illusion of controlled motion that was uncanny.

Reno's smile was self-deprecating. "I guess you'd have to call that my baseball period."

"Baseball?"

"Yeah." He shrugged, took a deep breath. "I used to play a little. I was a pitcher, so I didn't play every day. Left me quite a bit of time for whittling—you know, sittin' on the bench in the dugout...long nights on the road."

Jenna was frowning at the figure in her hands, which she now realized was a baseball player preparing to throw a ball. And suddenly she saw Reno without his shirt, throwing pebbles against a backdrop of white sand, cobalt sky and aquamarine blue. "This is what you were doing," she said, looking up at him in wonder. "Isn't it? That day at the beach? You were pitching."

He came toward her, laughing, his eyes shining like water in moonlight. "You mean you didn't know? Darlin', don't you know anything at all about baseball?"

"Well, I—" She shook her head regretfully. "Not really, I guess. I'm sorry."

"You mean..." He took her face in his hands and looked down into her eyes with heartstopping and bewildering intensity. "You've never heard of Babe Ruth...Ty Cobb...Joe DiMaggio?"

Jenna snorted indignantly. "Well of course I've *heard* of them. I'm not illiterate."

"Hmm." Reno's eyes narrowed. "How about Sandy Koufax...Tom Seaver...Nolan Ryan...Nathan Wells?"

She shook her head, looking bewildered. But inside Nate all hell was breaking loose, like Yankee Stadium on the Fourth of July. She really didn't know!

"Never mind," he said huskily, shaking with silent laughter, and pulled her into his arms. "It's not important. It was a long time ago...."

"But," Jenna persisted in a voice he could barely hear, her arms a stubborn barrier between them, "It was important to you, wasn't it?"

Nate stared down into her eyes for a dozen heartbeats, then looked up at the ceiling and let his breath out in a long slow sigh of surrender. "Yeah," he said quietly, unconsciously kneading her shoulders as the familiar wave of grief surged through him. "It was important to me. When I was a kid, baseball was just about the only thing that was im- portant to me. It was my ticket out."

"Out?" she whispered, not understanding. "Out of where?"

His laugh was harsh. "Out of where I was. Out of the mountains. Out of a life of doing the same thing my grandpa had done—which was breaking horses, by the way—and living in a nowhere town where nothing had ever happened or was ever going to happen—"

He stopped, then laughed again, softly this time, and with an old sadness. His hands relaxed their grip on her shoul- ders and began to stroke and caress instead. "The truth is, darlin', I was ashamed of who I was and where I came from. Ashamed that my shoes had holes in the soles and that my jeans had patches. Ashamed of not having indoor plumb- ing and electric light. I figured I deserved better than what two old people could give me with their hard work and sweat, and the way I saw it, I had one shot at getting it. You see, my grandpa taught me two things—besides how to ride a horse, that is. He taught me how to make things with my hands, and he taught me how to throw a baseball harder and faster than anybody else. He used to brag that I could throw a baseball through a knothole in a barn door."

Nate chuckled and shook his head. "I don't know if it was the bragging that did it, but I managed to attract enough attention to get a college scholarship. My second year in college, I got picked in the third round of the major-league draft. Before I knew it, before I was even out of my teens, I was standing out on a pile of dirt in front of fifty thousand screaming people, facing a ten-year veteran on his way to his third-hundred-RBI season. I was scared to death."

"What happened?" Jenna asked in an awed whisper, her skin prickling even though she didn't understand half of what he was saying.

His smile was crooked. "I threw three fastballs right by him—struck him out. Next time up he put my first pitch into the centerfield seats—a three-run homer. I went back to the minor leagues and learned how to throw a curveball and a change. The next year I was back up to stay. At least..." He shrugged and watched his hands slide over Jenna's shoulders, down her arms and back up again, then inward to the back of her neck.

She could feel the tension and emotion vibrating through his body and into the air that surrounded them, filling her head with a strange, subaudible thrumming. She moved her hands outward across his chest and down the smooth convexity of biceps and finally brought them to rest at his elbows. When her fingers found the tiny scars there, she felt his hands tighten involuntarily on the nape of her neck. She swallowed, fighting desperately against the aching pressure of understanding that was building inside her.

"But . . . you still miss it, don't you?" she whispered.

For uncounted seconds the thrumming grew stronger, the pressure inside her building to unbearable pitch. And then Reno suddenly let go a breath he'd been holding forever and caught her to him so hard she felt the trembling of controlled violence inside him. In a voice she'd never heard before, a voice like torn cloth, he said, "Darlin', there's not a day goes by that I don't miss it. Sometimes I dream about it at night—I hear the roar of the crowd, smell the fresh-cut infield grass. . . . I think the smells are what get to me most. Sometimes a certain smell, like the smell of an old saddle, just like the leather and sweat smell of a baseball glove . . . and I'm right back there again, just like it was yesterday."

The pressure inside Jenna exploded suddenly in a chaos of emotions that ricocheted and rebounded inside her like fireworks in a closed room. The havoc was terrifying, but the illumination made everything stunningly clear.

This was no Black Knight she held in her arms, nor Merlin, nor any other fantasy. He was a man, flesh and blood, muscle and bone, with laughter and tears, dreams and disappointments, faults and feelings. He was no magic healer, either, a heart mender she could use for her own selfish needs. He was a man capable of loving and of having his own heart broken.

Nancy was wrong. Whether or not Jenna McBride was happy was *not* the only thing that mattered. Reno mattered. Reno mattered to *her*, more than she'd thought he possibly could. He mattered so much she couldn't even comprehend it, except to know that it hurt her as much as if one of those careening missiles had pierced her heart.

She made a sharp, anguished sound. Reno rasped, "Jenny—" and stifled the cry with his mouth, as if he, too, had finally had more than he could endure. Her mouth opened under his; the sound became a deep-throated growl. She stood on tiptoe, lifting herself to the hungry thrusts of his tongue with a passion that bordered on desperation.

"Jenny—darlin'—" He tore his mouth from hers and held her tear-wet face between his hands. "What is it, love? Tell me what's wrong." His voice was harsh and ragged with concern, his eyes black and shining, like rain-wet streets.

"I—" she said, and stopped. *No!* she thought in panic and horror at what she'd almost said. But she couldn't say it! She couldn't say "I love you" to Reno because it just wasn't true. It would be the rebound emotions talking. It couldn't be the real thing. Nancy was right—her emotions were a mess. She was in no shape to tell real ones from fantasies. She couldn't cheat Reno by telling him such a lie. She *couldn't*.

She closed her eyes, drew a shuddering breath and whispered something that wasn't a lie. "Reno, I'm frightened."

His eyes softened and the creases deepened at their corners. "No need to be," he said gently, misunderstanding. "I told you, nothing happens until you want it to." He tried a grin, but it slipped awry. "Hey, I didn't tell you that sob story to get you to feel sorry for me, if that's what you're thinkin'." Serious again, he thumbed away tears and murmured, "Darlin', the only thing that matters here is how you feel about this. If you're not ready—"

"No!" Jenna shouted, pushing away from him, "that's not the only thing that matters! Damn it, I wish people would quit telling me that!" Wrenching herself from Reno's restraining hands she stormed blindly out of the cabin and slammed the door behind her.

Ten

Nate found her down by the creek, sitting on a carpet of live-oak mulch, throwing twiggy litter into the water with short, jerky motions. She stopped and looked up at him when she heard his footsteps.

"Hello, Gingerbread Lady," he said softly.

After a moment she said "Hi," and gave him kind of an embarrassed smile. It made his belly twist and writhe to see the tear tracks on her cheeks.

"Well, thank the Lord," he drawled as he hunkered down beside her and leaned over to touch her smile briefly with his. "I wasn't sure I was ever going to see that again." He sat back and got comfortable, with his arms draped across his drawn-up knees, then gave her a quick sideways look. "For a minute there, I thought I was looking at that little lost lady who came walking into the wolves' den last Friday night."

"I'm sorry." She looked down, then away, anywhere but at him. "I shouldn't have yelled at you like that. I don't know what got into me. But I'm fine now—really."

Yeah, sure, Nate thought, about as fine as I am. The creek slipped by his feet, muttering in commiseration. After a while he cleared his throat and said, "You know, what I thought then was that you looked like somebody running away from something. You feel like telling me what it is?"

Jenna looked at him finally, long and thoughtfully, then closed her eyes and took a quick breath, as if she'd just made some kind of decision. "It isn't what you think. It's nothing important—at least…well, I guess I thought it was, but now…" She shrugged, tried to smile. "Ridiculous as it seems, I was running away from the humiliation of Unrequited Love." The capitals were implicit and replete with self-mockery.

"I don't know," Nate drawled, stirring in the mulch between his feet with a stick, not smiling at all. "Seems to me there's not much that could hurt any worse than loving somebody who doesn't love you back."

He could feel her watching him with quiet, curious eyes. After a moment she whispered, "You sound as if you know."

Nate didn't answer. He wasn't sure whether his own love was unrequited or not, and he wasn't ready to put it to the test. He threw the stick into the creek, dusted off his hands and said briskly, "Tell me about it."

It wasn't as hard as she'd thought it would be. While she did shed a few tears when she got to the part about the decision to cut Jack Remington and everything associated with him out of her life, they were more from habit than anything, like the automatic lump in the throat when Bambi's mother dies.

Of course, she couldn't mention names, places and occupations, not without confessions and revelations she didn't want to make. But about the relationship itself she was unstinting, sparing neither Jack nor herself, resisting for once the automatic urge to explain, defend, rationalize, excuse.

So she was somewhat surprised, when she finished, to have Reno say thoughtfully, "Seems to me, it wasn't that he didn't love you so much as he *couldn't*. He's just not capable of it.'' She turned slowly to look at him. His eyes glittered back at her, jet black and hard as diamonds. "If the man didn't want to touch you, there's something wrong with him.''

It wasn't that the thought was new to Jenna; Nancy had said almost the same thing only a couple of days before, and Jenna had said it to herself more times than she cared to count, in anger, pain, bewilderment. But for some reason, only at that moment did she finally know it...feel it... believe it. The chuckling creek and all the other noises of a warm springtime afternoon faded away, leaving her alone with the new and beautiful stillness inside her. She felt a strange *loosening*, as if someone had just let go of the strings that held her up, and she waited in breathless suspense to see if she would fall. But instead there was warmth, a sense of new things growing, blossoming. She felt intense happiness and, bewilderingly, an urge to cry.

At last she drew a tremulous breath and said, "Yes. I think...I know that. And right now, more than anything else, I just feel sorry for him.''

It was true, she realized, listening to her own words with bemusement and wonder. It was true—the pain she'd carried around with her for so long was gone. Nancy had been right about one thing: Reno was her heart mender. For the first time in months she felt whole again. When she tried to recall the roller-coaster ride of her relationship with Jack, tried to tune in on the exhilaration and anguish, joy and uncertainty, self-doubt and despair, all she got were memories. Some were beautiful, some poignant, some bitter, some sad, but they were only memories; when she leaned on them, testing for the pain, she felt nothing. *Nothing at all*.

So what was this new ache inside her? This weakness and trembling...this terrible longing? Why did she still feel such an overpowering desire to have Reno's arms around her? She sat mute, just looked at him, needing him desperately, wanting him to touch her, silently crying out to him with all her might—surely he must hear her!

And then she saw something in the black depths of his eyes, something she'd never seen there before: uncertainty, wariness, fear. And in the glow of an insight that was totally new to her, Jenna realized that he was *afraid* to touch her. Hard on the heels of that came another new emotion—a wave of tenderness that washed through her like a flash flood and lodged in an aching mass in her throat.

"Reno," she whispered, "please hold me."

His reply was rough and scratchy, beautiful to her ears. "Darlin', that's all I've been wantin' to hear."

He touched her shoulder almost shyly, then slipped his hand under her hair to cradle the back of her neck. Trembling, weak and fragile as a newborn kitten, she crept into his arms. She felt him sigh as those big, strong arms closed around her; a warm masculine smell enveloped her; his hand covered her ear, shutting out the world. Never before in all her insulated, overprotected life could Jenna recall feeling so safe, so cherished, so loved.

Once again those bewildering waves of emotion rocked her, powerful and immutable as earth's own tremors. The sob she'd been holding back for so long shuddered through her, and though she closed her eyes as tightly as she could, the tears seeped through anyway and soaked into the fabric of Reno's T-shirt.

"Shh," he murmured, his voice deep and tender. "Jenny..."

He hadn't thought it was possible to feel so much. So much, it hurt. He hadn't thought he could hurt so much just because she did, so much he wanted to kill the one responsible for hurting her and spend the rest of his life making sure she never hurt again. It scared him, because he couldn't understand how it could have happened so quickly. He thought it must have been fate or some kind of miracle that had made her walk into that joint on the one night he'd decided to go hear old Ernie Rose and his band. When he thought about all the reasons he might not have gone that night, he got a cold, squeezing sensation in his chest. The realization that he might not have found this lady but for pure dumb luck scared the hell out him. The idea that he might lose her somehow scared him even more. So he tightened his arms around her, threaded his fingers through her silky, clean hair and drew in a great breath, filling his lungs with air and his heart with resolve. He wasn't going to lose her. Not if he could help it.

"Hello, darlin'," he rasped as Jenna sniffed and stirred, rubbing her face against the wet spot in the middle of his chest. He knew his voice sounded like a cattle stampede down a gravel road, and clearing his throat didn't help. "Feelin' better?"

She nodded, then pulled back a little and looked up at him, searching his face with her tear-bright eyes, looking both puzzled and hopeful, as if she thought he might have the answer to something of grave importance if only she knew the question.

"Do you want to go home?" Nate asked softly. "I'll take you if you do. Just say the word."

"No," she whispered, never taking her eyes from his face, "I don't want to go home." There was a long, sweet silence, and then, "I want you to make love to me."

It was funny, he thought, hearing her say those words, remembering what he'd said to her that first night and how glib and confident he'd been, to realize how much things had changed inside him since then. He didn't feel confident now. He felt fragile and exposed, scared as that teenage rookie who'd taken the mound against a steely-eyed veteran. Only for some reason this time he couldn't seem to find the old bravado to hide behind. Never let 'em know when they've got you on the ropes—hadn't that always been his motto? Well, here he was, on the ropes, with his guard down and the game on the line, and no idea what his next pitch was going to be.

"Jenny..." He brushed the backs of his fingers across her cheek and on into her hair, combing it behind her ear, looking hard into her still-drenched eyes all the while. Her mouth looked bruised. "Are you sure that's what you want?"

He'd wanted her so badly and for so long—only a matter of days, he supposed, though it seemed much longer to him. Almost, he thought, as if he'd been wanting her all of his life. His whole body was aching with the physical needs he'd been suppressing—more or less—since Saturday, but that wasn't what had him strung tighter than one of Ernie Rose's fiddle strings. It was this need to connect with her on more than just a physical level, which was something he'd never felt before, for any woman. He didn't just want her making love with him, he wanted her *loving* him. He wanted her eyes shining with it and the words on her lips when he finally entered her.

"Yes," she whispered, "I'm sure. Please...make love to me."

And still he went on searching her eyes, looking for the thing he wanted so badly. But it was like trying to see to the bottom of a wind-riffled pond.

She's not over him, he thought bleakly, shaking inside with anger and frustration. She was still hung up on him. The idea of Jenna wasting her tears on a guy like that—a nutcase, if you asked him—the guy had to have a few screws loose not to want what she had to give, and from the sound of it, she'd offered it all.

The anger surged up in him suddenly, taking him by surprise. Anger as elemental as fire, rising from the magma of primal memory; anger as primitive and uniquely masculine as the first challenge issued by one male to another.

It was a kind of madness. Before he knew he was going to, he was kissing her with single-minded purpose, as if with the imprint of his mouth on hers he would sear the memory of another man from her mind forever. He tangled his fingers in her hair and pulled her head roughly back. His mouth covered hers; his tongue forced her lips apart without waiting for her acquiescence and plunged deep in a raw and savage claiming. He ignored her shocked gasp; though with some sane part of him he heard the sound and knew he might be hurting or scaring her, it didn't seem important to him at that moment. All he wanted was to drive out all thoughts but those of him and with his mouth brand her, marking her irrevocably his.

She whimpered, a small, desperate cry that might have tempered his passion if she had not at the same moment opened her mouth under his and lifted herself to him as if the madness had claimed her, too. Her hands raked his shoulders and neck, tangled in his hair; her body arched and pushed upward in an unconscious seeking. The kiss became a savage dance of clashing teeth, bruising lips and mating tongues from which they finally had to tear themselves, hearts racing and breath gasping, like escapees from catastrophe.

Jenna cried out his name—"Reno!"—and that finally brought him back from the edge, though his mouth still surged hot and open over her bared throat, and he held her as if his life depended on it, shaking like a newborn colt. She said his name again, whispering this time. "Reno...please."

He murmured "Shh," automatically, while he tried to quiet himself, holding them both as still as he could, listening to the ragged rhythms of their merging heartbeats. He knew it wasn't anger any longer that was driving his heart like a stampede, but desire, pure and simple. More than desire. He'd been without a woman for too long and he'd waited for *this* woman for too long—all of his life, it seemed—and his need was pushing against the boundaries of his control. He tried to remind himself that she was vulnerable, confused, that she didn't know what—or who—she wanted and that he could get hurt. But it didn't make any difference. His need was too great, and he was a fool.

"Come on," he muttered, slipping his hand under her elbows as he stood up, lifting her with him.

Jenna stared at him, dazed and uncomprehending. "Where are we going?" she asked, blinking and trembling like an awakened sleepwalker, afraid to let go of his arms, knowing she'd fall if she did.

"Where are we going?" He smiled—not the slow, sweet smile she loved, but crookedly, almost painfully—and hooking one arm around her waist and the other behind her knees, lifted her into his arms. "We're going to make love," he stated flatly as he shifted his hold and began to stride up the grassy, flower-carpeted slope. "I don't intend it to be on the ground."

His eyes... Jenna thought. They were so dark, so deep, the pain and need in them so plain to see that it frightened her. It wasn't a physical fear, though there might have been a little of that in her trembling legs and wildly racing heart. But that kind of fear seemed only natural and understandable to her, like the fear of riding on a motorcycle or of jumping out of an airplane for the very first time—a delicious, shivering fear made effervescent with excitement. *This* fear, though... this was different, something she'd never felt before. It was a cold emptiness, a strange, hollow feeling deep, deep inside. She felt like a small child, lost in the dark. Fragile, vulnerable... exposed.

Oh, God, she thought, watching Reno's face, the deepening creases at the corners of his eyes, the tiny muscle working in the hinge of his jaw. What's happening to me? It wasn't supposed to be like this. I wasn't supposed to feel like this! It was just supposed to be a fling. I can't love him. *I can't.*

Nate felt the gaze of her wide, frightened eyes on his face and tried with every ounce of self-control he had left to gentle himself, to slow himself down. Unless he was very much mistaken, he didn't think she'd had much experience with men, and the last thing in the world he wanted to do was scare her.

In the cabin doorway he paused and looked down at her. "Darlin', if you're thinking about changing your mind, this is the time to tell me. I'll take you home. Just say the word."

Her swallow was audible. "No," she whispered, "I haven't changed my mind. I don't want to go home."

Reno nodded, almost grimly, Jenna thought, and crossed the cabin in three long strides. He elbowed aside a curtain she hadn't noticed before and carried her into an alcove just big enough to accommodate a brass double bed. Inside, it was very dim and cool and quiet. She could hear her own heart beating.

"You're shaking," Reno murmured, lifting her a little and turning her body toward him.

She nodded, and whispered against the hollow of his throat, "I know. I can't seem to stop. It's all right, it doesn't mean anything."

It means you're nervous, he thought; maybe even scared. He was almost glad about the trembling. It was a constant reminder to him to go slowly with her. And with that in mind he sat down on the bed, cradled her in his lap and kissed her.

He's so gentle. Jenna's mind formed the thought out of chaos. While his tongue was bathing her mouth with deep, slow strokes, his agile fingers disposed of buttons and belt buckle, pulled shirttails free, pushed cloth aside and found naked flesh, passion hot and aching for his touch. Her breast seemed to fill his hand. She pressed closer, then tried to cringe away from the exquisite abrasion of his palm across her hardened nipple.

At last she had to tear her mouth from his with a shuddering gasp; she was overloaded with sensation—it was too much—she couldn't breathe. She was dizzy with sensation, tingling and burning in every part of her, unable to believe she could feel so much, terrified she might not survive it, wanting it never to stop. And still his hand stroked and kneaded her, now roughly... now so gently she arched into it, craving more.

With his arm supporting her shoulders he lifted and turned her toward him, giving her the haven of his chest and throat while his fingers peeled her jeans zipper down. His hand slipped under elastic and nylon and lay flat and warm in the taut hollow of her stomach, then pushed slowly down into the softness between her thighs.

Her breath exploded against his neck in what sounded almost like a sob. Without stopping the gentle stroking, Nate tightened his arm around her and brought his lips close to her ear. "Easy..." he whispered. "It's all right."

She shook her head, a small, distraught jerk. "There's...something I have to tell you. I haven't... oh—"

"Haven't what, Jenny love?"

"Haven't...done this before. I've never—"

"Never?" Tenderness was a slow, sweet blossoming inside him; a chuckle shook him like a small earthquake. "Now why doesn't that surprise me?"

"It's just—I'm afraid...."

"Don't be afraid."

"No—I'm afraid...." Her face, hot with embarrassment, sought the protected cove at the base of his neck. She drew in a quivering breath. "I'm afraid I won't know what to do."

"Ah, Jenny..." He closed his eyes and laid his cheek against her hair and stilled his fingers for a moment while he held her in that quiet intimacy. "Jenny, darlin', there's only two things you need to do."

"What?"

Tenderness roughened his voice. "Well, the first thing you can do is unlock your legs."

"Oh—" He felt her tense with chagrin, then abruptly relax. Her silent laughter joined his. "Okay, I can do that," she whispered, and did, though he felt her legs tremble. "What else?"

"Just...trust me." He drew an unsteady breath and held her as closely as he could while he slipped his finger between her soft folds. "Yeah...like that. Like that...ah, Jenny..."

Her body tightened, then to his delight began to move slowly and sinuously against the pressure of his hand. "Yes..." he whispered, and deepened the caress. Shudders rocked her; he absorbed them and pushed deeper still, searching for the molten center of her body. She was so hot, so tight...he wanted her enfolding him like a fine, soft glove, more than he'd ever wanted anything in his life, but he couldn't...he didn't dare...not yet. His muscles quivered with the strain of self-control.

Jenna's body was beyond her control. She'd given it up to this man called Reno, a man she barely knew but trusted with all her heart and soul, the man whose arms held her so safely and securely while his hands did incredible things to her body... drawing fire from her depths and spreading it like sunshine over her skin, coaxing waves of silvery ripples through her muscles, retiming her rhythms, refocusing her senses until she was aware of nothing, nothing in the world but her body and his hands. *Magical hands...*

The sensation intensified, the rhythms accelerated, like a locomotive running out of control. It was too much—she couldn't bear it—she had to stop it! She tried to stop it, tried to slow it down, but she might as well have tried to halt a train by dragging her foot. Finally, with a high, frightened cry, she clutched at Reno's shoulders and hid her face against his neck, bracing for catastrophe.

"It's all right... it's all right." His voice was a lifeline, a hand to hold in the dark. She clung to it while all hell broke loose inside her, still dimly aware that his hand housed the fragile, pulsing center of her body in warmth and safety. "Easy, darlin'... shh."

He held her while she cooled and quieted, until he felt awareness returning, bringing with it a touch of shyness, the beginnings of embarrassment. Then he laughed softly and murmured, "Hey, don't curl up on me now. Open up, darlin'... that's right."

She gave a breathy laugh that tickled his neck and relaxed her legs enough to allow him to shuck her jeans and panties down and off. Then he set about soothing and gentling her, stroking the long, smooth curve of hip and back, taut belly and soft inner thighs and the moist curls at their juncture. He soothed her with words, too, meaningless, murmured phrases and endearments that had never come naturally to him before, until she began to move again with the unconscious voluptuousness of a cat being petted. Until finally, lying open and unselfconsciously naked in his arms, she opened her eyes and gazed up at him.

"I know there's more," she murmured. Her face looked moist and flushed, her eyes troubled. "I'm not sure...."

"Oh, there's more." He made his chuckle easy, belying the need that was pounding like a gong in his belly. "We'll get to it...in good time. No hurry..."

But there was already a fever in her skin, a sleepy, sexy look in her eyes. He'd forgotten what a fast learner she was.

She lifted her hand and touched his face, a feathery touch, full of wonder. She traced the creases beside his eyes and around his mouth, the hard, bony edge of his jaw and the satiny smoothness of his lips. Her palm measured the pulse in his neck, slipped over his collarbone and down inside his shirt, stretching and pulling the soft fabric aside. She closed her eyes and with a sigh, pressed her open mouth to his chest.

"Here, darlin', let me..." The words vibrated pleasantly against her lips. She felt his body flex and tighten as he hauled the shirt up and over his head. And then her hands were on him once more, kneading hard muscle and tiny, pebbled nipples while her mouth explored his body the way she'd learned to do that afternoon on the beach, with the sun on her back and the wind in her hair and his skin sweat slicked and salty. As she had then, she lost herself in the pure, sensual pleasure of his body, loving the way he smelled and tasted, the way his muscles tightened and quivered when her mouth touched them, the groan that seemed to come from the bottom of his soul.

"My God, Jenny...you play rough."

"Yes," she whispered smugly, warming him with her breath, "I know. But I want this...off." Her tongue traced the edge of his jeans while her hands tugged futilely at his belt buckle.

He chuckled, delighted at her boldness, and took a moment to oblige her, but when she'd have touched him with her hands and mouth he caught her wrists and held them. "No, baby," he said gently, "I can't let you do that."

She licked her lips and looked at him with dazed, questioning eyes. "Why not?"

Still holding her wrists captive, he rolled her onto her back and raised himself above her, bracing himself on his hands, feeling the tension in her muscles, the fragility of her bones. "Because," he growled, and closed his eyes. He didn't want to tell her he'd never been so full or so hard, that he wasn't sure how much longer he was going to be able to control himself and that he had to be able to control himself if he was going to keep from hurting her. "Jenny," he whispered hoarsely, "let me go slowly, darlin'. You said you've never done this before. You do know it's not apt to feel very good. I'll try not to hurt you—"

"It's all right, I remember what you told me." Her words were slurred and slightly drunken. Nate opened his eyes and looked down at her, and found that she was smiling.

"Told you . . . what?"

"When you were teaching me to ride your motorcycle. You said—" her eyelids drifted down; her body stirred sinuously beneath him "—you said, 'The more you relax, the easier it is for me. The more you go with me, the better it is for both of us. Just like makin' love. . . .' "

"I said that?" he whispered wonderingly.

"Oh yes."

"And you remembered?"

"I remembered. . . ."

He leaned over and kissed her . . . deeply, slowly, tenderly. Shifting his legs and hers to make a place for himself, he brought his hips against hers and then rested there a moment in the cradle of her body. She felt his heat and hardness pressing against her, the power and weight of his body on hers, and accepted them without fear. Her own body felt moist, humid . . . ready. It knew what it needed and knew, too, that whatever pain there might be simply didn't matter.

He slipped his hand between their bodies and found her hot and swollen. Sliding one finger inside her, he used her body's own lubricant to moisten himself, making it easier for her. He reached under her, lifted her hips slightly and began with exquisite care to enter her.

She felt it first as pressure and then as burning. Her muscles tensed, her chest lifted.... *Relax.* But a single, involuntary cry escaped her anyway when her body's barriers gave way, and Reno quickly lowered his head to kiss her and whisper brokenly, "Easy, darlin'... easy."

She closed her eyes tightly and nodded. As he pushed slowly into her, there was a tightness and pressure...and the most extraordinary sense of completion, of rightness, of being filled to bursting with feelings too powerful to contain. Tears squeezed between her eyelids and ran down into her hair.

"I'm not crying," she whispered when Reno wordlessly touched the tears with his lips. "It's just that there's so much inside me...."

"I know...I know." His body shook slightly with rueful laughter. "In me, too. Jenny, you feel so good...too good. I'm afraid I can't hold back much longer. Are you ready? Then...come with me, darlin'. Move with me, now...like we're one body."

"Like dancin'," she whispered, and he remembered that he'd once said something like that to her, too.

And then for a while he didn't remember or think about anything at all, including the need to be gentle.

Rocked to the depths of her being, Jenna held him, felt his powerful body surging into hers, felt his back and buttocks muscles clench and tighten with the spasms of release, and felt as if she were soaring. It was like the day he'd taken her flying on the back of his motorcycle—first the nervousness and anticipation, the fear...and then surprise, wonder, excitement, exhilaration, the feeling it was what she'd been meant to do all along. And finally, sheer, unadulterated joy. But this was *more.* So much more. The joy she felt was different, at once quieter and more intense, a fierce and primal elation that was tangled up somehow with things like pride and protectiveness, strength and tenderness...love.

Love. That's what this is, she thought, dazed but absolutely certain. She loved him. No matter what it had started out to be, no matter what she'd intended, it had happened, and that was that. She loved him.

"Ah, Jenny..." Reno's breath gusted warmly in the hollow of her neck as he sighed and relaxed, letting his weight rest on her for just a moment. "I never meant to do that."

Jenna murmured, "No?" and went on stroking his back, lightly grazing his skin with her nails.

"No." He shifted his weight to one side and raised himself on one elbow, but didn't separate from her. His face looked strained, his eyes worried and dark. "I meant to be more gentle. Are you all right?"

"Yes, I'm fine," she said, surprised and pleased to discover that it was true; except for a certain throbbing, there was almost no discomfort. In fact... She moved experimentally under him, just a small undulation of hips and pelvis...and felt a delicious warmth spread outward from the union of their bodies, into her belly and thighs. She let her hand glide slowly downward, into the small of his back, up and over one smooth buttock...and felt it tense and tighten. Her hand moved on over one hard-edged hip, discovered the silky place at the top of his thigh, the thicket of damp, springy hair....

"Hey," Reno said, his laughter bumping against her hand, "what do you think you're doing?" He glanced down, then gave her a look of wonder. His slow, sweet smile spread over his face as he leaned down to kiss her. "Later, darlin'," he said, his voice low and husky. "Give us both a little time to recuperate." He moved as if to separate himself from her.

"No!" Jenna cried, holding him fiercely, almost with panic. "Not yet—hold me a little longer...please."

"As long as you want me to, darlin'. But I just need to—there...that's better." He rolled onto his side and rearranged their legs so that now he cradled her, and it was his hands that traveled slowly and gently up and down her back.

"Hmm," Jenna sighed, snuggling closer, "that's nice. I think I could stay like this forever."

"Do you have to go home tonight?" Reno asked, lifting his head to press a kiss on the top of her head.

Jenna was still for a moment, thinking of Nancy and her warnings and reservations and objections. "No," she said. "I don't have to go home."

"In that case—" he reached out, caught the edge of the comforter and twitched it over her "—forever's yours," he growled softly, "if you want it."

Forever. Why didn't that frighten her? But it was the thought of separating from him that frightened her, as much as the thought of losing a part of her own body. One body...wasn't that what he'd said? But, Jenna thought, they weren't one body at all, they were two very different bodies only temporarily conjoined—hers soft and smooth and fair, with a few freckles where the sun touched it; his hard-muscled and tanned and lightly furred with hair. In a little while they'd separate and move around quite independently of each other—and that was only natural and right. The alternative was ludicrous.

"What's funny?" Reno asked sleepily.

"Nothing," Jenna whispered. "I'm just...thinking."

You're a part of me, she thought. Not of my body, but something much, much more. You're a part of *me*, of my heart and my soul.

And she shivered in his arms. Because she wondered if she should lose him, whether all the heart menders in the world could ever mend the hole he would leave in her.

Eleven

Jenna was standing in the cabin doorway, wearing one of Nate's old blue work shirts and not much else. Her feet and legs were bare, her hair finger-combed to an artless disarray. The early spring sunshine poured in around her, sifting reddish highlights through her hair and giving her outline an almost ethereal glow. Watching her, Nate wondered how he could ever have thought she wasn't beautiful.

"What's that?" she asked suddenly, her hair swinging across her cheek as she cocked her head to a listening angle.

Nate turned his attention back to the eggs he was scrambling, just in time to avoid disaster, then dumped the steaming lot onto a plate and the frying pan into the sink and went to join her. "What's what?" he murmured, wrapping his arms around her from behind and gathering her close.

She leaned back with a blissful sigh and a sinuous little wiggle that nestled her bottom delightfully in the fork of his thighs. Then she went still, head turned, listening again. "That—hear it?"

"Quail," Nate mumbled. "Down in the creek bed. What the hell do you think you're doing?" What she was doing was moving again, arousing him in a way he wouldn't have thought possible after the way they'd spent the last twelve hours or so.

"Quail? Really?" She was teasing him—he could hear the sultry little smile in her voice. And feel the full, firm imprint of her bottom burning through the unforgiving barrier of his jeans. "Do you ever see them? Are there a lot of them? Do you think—"

"What are you," he growled as he lowered his mouth to the side of her neck, "some kind of animal lover?"

"Yes, as a matter of fact . . ." But her voice was growing weaker because Nate was blowing his warm breath all up and down the taut cords of her neck, and his arm was holding her pinned against his chest while his palm massaged one taut nipple through blue chambray. Although she tried, gamely. "And, um . . . that reminds me . . . ." He flipped the shirttails roughly aside and pressed his hand to the lower part of her body, bringing her hard against him. And her voice died completely in a soft, breathless gasp.

But when he pushed his fingers into her soft curls and found the delicate, swollen place between her thighs, her gasp was sharp and somewhat surprised.

"Yeah, you see?" Nate murmured as he withdrew his hand, turned her and folded her into his arms. "You're already sore, darlin'. I don't want to cripple you."

"You don't need to protect me," she whispered against his neck. "I'm a big girl, I know what I'm doing."

Nate sighed and held her tighter, laying his cheek against her hair. She'd said almost the same thing last night, and he'd let it go at that, but he didn't feel good about it. Not that he objected to the idea of Jenna pregnant with his child, but there were still too many things that weren't right between them. So many things he didn't know or understand.

"Don't make it so hard for me," he said, and reminded her gently, "You were going to say something."

"What?" She pulled back and looked at him, her forehead wrinkling with the effort to remember. "Oh, yes—I was going to ask you, where in the world are the dogs?"

Nate became very still, except for the pulse throbbing in his belly. "Dogs?"

"Yes, you told me you had dogs, remember? The other night when we were having dinner. And I was wondering...I hadn't seen any sign of them, and I wondered where they were."

"Ah," Nate said. "The dogs." He ran his hands lightly down her back, over the round swell of her bottom and back up again to her shoulders, took a deep breath and eased her away from him. "I imagine they're all down at the big house. The men have been working cattle, and they like to be in on that." It comforted him some that as far as it went it was the truth. He could still tell himself that except for his name and a few omissions, he hadn't really lied to her. He didn't like lying to her.

For a long moment he hesitated, rubbing the hollows in front of her shoulders with his thumbs. Then he gave her a quick kiss and let go of her. "Come on, darlin', let's eat this before it gets cold. I've got to get you home before your friend calls out the search-and-rescue squad."

"Oh, it's all right," Jenna said lightly, "I told her not to worry if I didn't come home." But her eyes slid away from him, and he noted a faint flush on her cheeks. "And anyway, she'll be at the library by this time."

"The library?"

"Yes, that's where she works."

"Ah." He handed her a plate and they sat down together on the couch. They ate cold scrambled eggs and leathery toast in a silence that had an edge to it, a constraint that hadn't been there before. Nate wasn't sure what had caused it, but it seemed to be mutual. Each of them was holding something back—he knew it and for his part at least, deeply regretted doing it. It was time for the walls to come down, but damned if he knew how to make it happen. He knew he ought to just tell her straight out that his name wasn't Reno, that his real one was practically a household word and that he owned this ranch and most of the land as far as you could see on a clear day. He wasn't sure why he didn't, except that he'd already revealed so much of himself to her, and she'd given him so little in return. He felt as if he were standing out in the open, exposed and vulnerable, while she was still hiding, safe behind cover. He needed her to give him something—not a lot, not everything all at once, he was a patient man. But *something*, a part of herself that would let him know she was coming to trust him and that this wasn't all just on one side.

The quail were still singing their monotonous songs. When Jenna asked, Nate identified a mourning dove for her, too, and then, half joking, he asked her where she'd been all her life that she'd never heard a mourning dove's cry. She looked sad for a moment, then thoughtful.

"I don't know," she said finally. "I've done a lot of traveling, mostly in . . . cities. I guess I've seen a lot of different places, but I don't . . ." She drew in a breath that seemed painful to her. "I don't think I've *done* very much. Up till now, I've spent most of my life—" She paused, and when she smiled and said, "—imagining things," Nate knew it wasn't what she'd meant to say. Then she looked down at the cold toast in her hand and took another of those difficult breaths. "I'm not brave or venturesome. The fact is, I'm not a very interesting person."

Nate didn't say anything for a moment. Then he stood up, took her plate and his and put them in the sink. He reached for her hand. "Come 'ere," he said roughly, "I want to show you something."

He towed her over to the table and twitched the cover off the thing he'd been working on for the last few days, then stood back and let her look. His heart was hammering under his ribs with something that felt like stage fright; even as a kid he'd never liked anyone to see what he was doing until he'd finished it. He hadn't known until that moment that he was going to show it to Jenna, and right now he felt stark naked and vulnerable as a newborn baby.

"Well," he said finally, his voice raw with unnamed emotions, "what do you think?"

The silence and the suspense seemed unbearable, until at last Jenna turned to him, her face both awed and puzzled. "It's me, isn't it? But I don't—I don't look like that. Do I?"

"Yeah, you do." Nate wrapped his arms around her and pulled her back against him, just because he needed the solid reassurance of her in his arms. And realized only then that they were both vibrating with deep, inner tremors. "You get that look sometimes. I noticed it the first night I met you."

It was only a bust, something he'd never tried before, less than life-size, with the head slightly turned and tilted, windblown strands of hair across the face. But with that angle of the head and with a certain tilt to the mouth and attitude of chin, he'd tried to capture the essence of that daredevil spark that always excited him so.

Jenna shook her head, laughing a little. "But she looks so mischievous. So brave. And I'm not. I never have been."

"The hell you're not." Nate tightened his arms around her and pressed his face hard against the side of hers, as if he could physically squeeze the belief into her. "That—" he jerked his head toward the clay figure "—is you."

"But I'm the Gingerbread Lady, remember? I ran away!"

Nate shook his head. "You walked away, darlin'. There's a big difference between walking and running. Sometimes it takes more guts to walk than it does to hang on to something that's no good for you."

The words left an ache in his chest. He listened to their harsh echo in the silence while he held her, swaying a little, back and forth. And then she turned suddenly, put her arms around his neck and buried her face in the warmth of his neck. It was a few moments before he realized that she was crying.

"You're going to do *what*?" Nancy said in an outraged whisper. Remembering where she was, she flashed the pink-faced, white-haired man in blue seersucker a perfunctory smile as she deftly scanned the computer code and tucked a card into the pocket of the last book in his pile. "There you are, sir, have a nice day!" she muttered as she rounded the corner of the counter and took Jenna by the arm. "You're going back to L.A. to see *Jack*? For God's sake, *why*?"

Jenna allowed herself to be steered into the intermediate-children's section, which was deserted at that hour on a school day, with good humor. Nothing could disturb her this morning, not even Nancy at her bossiest and most meddlesome.

"I have some business to discuss with Jack Remington," she said with a patient smile. "That's all. And I can't really do it over the telephone."

Nancy frowned. "Business?"

"Yes." Jenna's smile became a little gulp of suppressed excitement. All that had happened, all that was in her heart, was churning around like trapped effervescence, ready to explode. "I'm going to tell Jack I'll go ahead with the show... *if* he promises to do me a favor in return."

"A favor? What favor? Jen, are you sure you should do this? You just got free of that man, and now you're walking right back into the same situation. You'll just be opening yourself up all over again for more hurt—"

"No," Jenna said with conviction, "not the same situation. I can handle Jack Remington. I'm not going to get hurt. Don't worry about me, Nancy, I'm going to be fine. More than fine—I'm just... great." She gave her a quick, breathless hug. "But I have to do just this one thing. It's important."

"What's so important," Nancy said, still looking unhappy, "that you're willing to risk all the progress you've made these last few days? I don't understand."

Jenna smiled, hugging to herself the wonderful idea that had come to her when she'd first held Reno's carved wooden lion in her hands. But for now it and everything else about Reno, the way she felt about him, were all too new and too precious to share. "I can't tell you now," she said, giving her best friend another quick hug, half apology, half promise. "Not until I've worked everything out. But I'll call you soon, I promise. Nancy—thanks... for everything."

"You've changed," Nancy said slowly. "I don't know what it is, but in the last few days, you've really..."

"Grown up?" Jenna said, laughing because Nancy was looking wary, as if she didn't know quite what to make of her. "Yes, I guess maybe I have—at last."

"Is it... Reno? Is that what's done this?"

"Well..." Jenna's smile turned inward, filling her with warm, golden light. "I think he may have had something to do with it."

"Then it was the right thing to do, I guess—having this little fling—wasn't it?"

"Yes," Jenna said softly, "I guess it was."

She squeezed her best friend's hand and left her standing there among the stacks of books, looking worried and most uncharacteristically uncertain.

"I'm sorry," said the cool, detached voice on the telephone, "Jenna isn't here."

Nate carefully moved a ledger out of the way and sat down on the corner of his desk. "Okay...listen, this is Reno. When do you expect her back?"

There was a pause. "Well, umm...actually, she won't be back. She's gone home—to L.A."

"I see." Nate could feel his jaw tensing up and made a conscious effort to relax it.

Apparently discomfited by his silence, the woman on the other end of the line finally broke it with a nervous cough. When she spoke, there was a note of pity in her voice that grated on his ears. "She was only here for a short visit, you know."

"Yeah," Nate said. "Right." He took a deep breath. "Listen, do you have a number where I can reach her?"

"I'm sorry, I really don't think I should give out that information."

Impersonal as a recording, Nate thought. "Look," he shouted, as his own frustration finally broke down his control, "I'm not asking for state secrets, here, I just want to talk to her!"

There was another pause, and then the voice said gently, "I would think if she'd wanted to talk to you, she'd have given you her number herself, don't you?"

Nate swore and hung up.

Damn woman, he thought. Some sort of misguided watchdog. He sat still, staring at the telephone while a knot of cold formed in his belly and spread outward from there into every part of his being.

Presently, the cold drove him outdoors, where the last rays of the setting sun were splashing across the hilltops, turning the new spring green to autumn gold. The dogs came wagging up to him, leaning against his legs and pushing their muzzles into his hands. Nate rubbed and scratched and patted and accepted moist demonstrations of canine affection in return, but the cold inside him remained.

Something's wrong, he thought. She wouldn't have left like that, not without a word. He couldn't believe it of her. Not Jenna.

But this morning she'd cried in his arms and hadn't been able to tell him why.

He needed to talk to her. Somehow he had to convince that dragon of a friend of hers to tell him where he could find her. He didn't seem to be having much luck on the telephone, but if he could just get her face-to-face.

He thought he remembered that Jenna had told him her friend worked at a library. A few phone calls.... He looked at his watch. Too late to do anything tonight. He took a deep breath and let it out slowly, wiggling his shoulders to ease the tension. *Tomorrow....*

He stuck his hands in the back pockets of his jeans and walked slowly to the edge of the porch, just as the sun slipped behind the hills, leaving only shadows.

* * *

It was five minutes past ten when Jenna pushed through the front doors of the Remington Art Gallery on Wilshire Boulevard in Beverly Hills. The receptionist gasped, "Miss McBride! I didn't—" and was halfway to her feet when Jenna waved her back to her seat.

"Good morning, Carla," she said briskly as she swept past. "Is Jack in his office?"

"Yes—yes, he is. Go right on up." The flustered girl sank into her chair and picked up the telephone. "I'll tell him you're here."

Jenna flashed her a smile and started up the spiral staircase to the second floor landing and the director's private offices. It was hard, climbing those stairs with the receptionist's avid and frankly speculative gaze on her, when her stomach felt hollow and her knees like sponges. But Jenna kept thinking of the small terra-cotta head on Reno's worktable, the girl with windblown hair and an air of reckless abandon. *Courage*, she thought as she knocked on, then pushed open the familiar door.

Jack Remington was sitting behind his desk, using it as he so often did to establish a barrier between himself and whoever else happened to be in the room. He looked as he always did, too: impossibly handsome, impossibly elegant, his eyes glowing with warmth that Jenna finally understood was only on the surface.

"Well, hello there, stranger." His voice was so pleasant, so musical; Jenna couldn't help but think of Reno's rough-and-scratchy drawl. "How are you?"

Incredible, she thought. It's as if nothing ever happened between us. As if all the things I said to him, the letter I wrote to him . . . never happened. Or didn't matter.

Courage. She took a deep breath and said without preamble, "Jack, I've just come to tell you that I'll do the show—"

"Hey, that's great. I knew—"

"—Under one condition."

"What's that?" He was still smiling, but there was a wary look in his dark blue eyes.

"There's a sculptor," Jenna said, the words tumbling out of her. "In the Santa Ynez Valley. He works mostly in wood, clay, some bronze. I want you to handle him—all three galleries."

"Well, now, Jenna, I'll always be happy to take a look at an artist if you think it's worth my time." His tone was austere, responding, finally, to the coolness in her. "But you know I can't promise any more than that, certainly not on just your recommendation." He stood up, the better to intimidate her with his height and bearing. "Those decisions are mine and always will be."

Jenna shook her head and stood her ground. "I want your promise that you will show him," she said softly but clearly, "or...you don't show me. There are other galleries, Jack."

"Jenna, I'm sorry, I can't—"

"Goodbye, Jack." She had her hand on the doorknob when he stopped her.

"Jenna, wait." She heard the soft hiss of anger, quickly controlled. "All right, listen, if he's as good as you say he is, I'll handle him. Fair enough?"

She turned slowly. "Fair enough."

"Your show's in two weeks."

"I'll be ready," Jenna breathed, and took the hand he offered her, bracing for the little jolt of electricity she'd always experienced at his touch. But there was nothing. It was just a hand, with no magic in it at all.

"When do I get to see this genius of yours?" Jack called as she left his office.

"I'll let you know," Jenna shot back as she all but flew down the staircase.

Half an hour later she was in her own car, heading north on the 101 Freeway toward Santa Barbara.

"Nancy?" The heavyset lady with the neat cap of salt-and-pepper hair and thick glasses smiled at Nate and pointed. "Yes, of course. There she is, right there."

Nate thanked her and ambled slowly along the counter, studying the woman who was sitting on a stool at the other end of it, thumbing through a thick reference book and making notes on a writing tablet. Petite, blond, pretty...not exactly his idea of a librarian—or a dragon lady.

Just opposite the blonde he stopped, leaned across the counter and drawled softly, "Excuse me . . . I think you and I need to have a talk."

His voice startled her so badly her pencil went skittering off across the tablet. She looked up and her eyes went wide, the expression in them making him feel as if he ought to turn around and see what sort of monster was standing behind him.

"Oh . . . God," she whispered, "you're—"

"Reno." He offered his hand across the counter and was a little surprised when she took it; the smile that went with it wasn't pleasant. "You want to talk to me here, or is there someplace we can go?"

A few minutes later he was in the library parking lot, facing her across the saddle of his bike. It was early afternoon and although the sun was trying hard to break through the murk, the day was still on the chilly side. But Nate was pretty sure that wasn't why the blonde was shivering. He hadn't meant to intimidate her, but he wasn't exactly in the mood for pleasantries.

"Listen, Reno," she said quickly before he could begin, "I know how you must feel—"

"Do you?" Nate muttered caustically. "I doubt it." He folded his arms and stared down at her, the same look he used to give a rookie batter right before he cut loose with a fastball on the inside part of the plate, the kind of pitch that made a batter suck in his breath and check to see if his belt buckle was still there.

Nate let out a long, slow breath, trying to ease the tension in his belly. "Look...Nancy. I'm just trying to get hold of Jenna. I don't know what she's told you—" He stopped there, because his feelings for Jenna weren't something he cared to discuss with a stranger. "I need to talk to her. All I need from you is a phone number."

The blonde hugged herself and looked unhappy. "I'm sorry. I just don't think I should give you that information without asking Jenna. If she didn't—"

"Then ask her, damn it!" Nate rasped, then just as quickly reined in his emotions. Nancy was looking scared but determined, and he knew he wasn't going to get anywhere with anger. He rubbed both hands over his face—he hadn't slept much and his eye sockets felt like burned-out holes—and said softly, "Just tell me one thing. Jenna said you were the one who told her to go out with me. And now you're trying to protect her from me. Mind tellin' me why?"

Nancy looked so miserable he almost felt sorry for her. "Jenna's my best friend," she whispered. "We—she didn't mean to hurt anyone." She closed her eyes and muttered, "Damn," then took a breath and faced him. "Reno, please try to understand. When Jenna came to visit me, she'd just gotten out of a very bad relationship. She was still hurting, on the rebound, really. She wasn't ready for anything...serious. Anything permanent. It was just...we thought—"

"You thought it would be okay, though, if she just had this little...fling with me, is that it?" Nate's voice cracked; he could feel the rage building like magma inside him. "A nice little affair, no strings? Well, lady, next time you decide to play games with my life, let me in on it, huh? You see, the thing is, nobody told me the rules!"

He doubled up his fists, then had to grab the handlebar grips to keep the rage and pain under control. It wasn't this woman's fault, he reminded himself; Jenna was a big girl and she'd made her own choices.

"I'm sorry," Nancy said again, still hugging herself like she was trying to keep warm. "She never meant to hurt anyone. I'm sorry if you misunderstood."

Nate just looked at her. The violence inside him required some sort of expression, so he stomped the starter and revved up the Harley's engine till it screamed. "Do me a favor, will you?" he shouted over the racket. "If you hear from Jenna, tell her I called." He patted down his pockets looking for something to write his phone number on, then muttered, "Ah, to hell with it!" and roared out of the parking lot.

He rode without a helmet, trying to let the wind do what no amount of self-discipline could—blow all thoughts and memories of Jenna out of his mind. It didn't work; he didn't really expect it to.

Long ago, The Game had taught him that a mistress could have two sides. Baseball, his first and—until now—his most unforgettable mistress, had given him the best and worst moments of his life.

And now . . . there was Jenna.

Twelve

———

Reno?'' The woman shook her lacquered, reddish-blond head. "Nope, nobody here by that name. I think you got the wrong house, hon. Sorry." She took a drag on her cigarette as she turned away.

Jenna cried, "Wait—please..." and opened her car door. The four dogs, who had retired to a cautious distance at the woman's sharp reprimand, stirred suspiciously and moved closer. They were a motley but competent-looking lot, and Jenna gave them a nervous glance as she shut the door behind her. "Please—I know this is the right place. I was just here yesterday. He said he worked here. Are you sure..."

The woman turned back, holding her broom and the cigarette in the same hand and frowning. She was wearing skintight jeans, a blue Western-style shirt and a silver Navaho belt, and in spite of the fact that she had to have been at least fifty, had hips as slim and trim as a boy's. To Jenna, she seemed as formidable as the dogs.

She looked Jenna up and down with a narrow-eyed stare while she took another long pull on her cigarette, then turned her head and bellowed, "Tom!"

A door slammed and a man came out onto the porch, carrying a cowboy hat in his hands. He had a round belly and skinny, badly bowed legs, and when he came down the steps it was sideways and with great care, as if the legs were stiff and perhaps even painful.

"Yeah, Twyla? Ma'am...." he murmured, nodding at Jenna. He had weathered skin and kind eyes, she thought. The top half of his forehead was pinkish white.

"Tom, have you hired on any new hands in the last day or two? This lady's lookin' for somebody named Reno. Says he told her he worked here. Any of the boys call himself that—a nickname, maybe?"

Tom scratched his stomach while he thought it over, then shook his head. "No...no, nobody like that here." He squinted at Jenna as he put on his hat. "Sorry, ma'am, looks like somebody either gave you a bum steer or you got the wrong place. Are you sure you got the right address?"

"I don't really have an address," Jenna said faintly. A terrible tightness was forming in her chest and her throat. "I just thought...I was sure this was the place."

"Well," Tom drawled sympathetically, "I know how it is. You can get turned around sometimes. All these hills and canyons and roads, they start to look alike."

"Yes," Jenna said, "I guess so. I'm very sorry I bothered you." She turned blindly and fumbled for the door handle of her car. "Thank you. I'm sorry...."

The trembling finally overtook her about the time she reached the main road. She pulled over and stopped, and for a long time sat gripping the steering wheel while waves of cold, sick fear rippled through her.

This is ridiculous, she thought, fighting a strange desire to laugh because she knew it would be only one step from laughter to tears. She couldn't have lost him! Not like this, not over a stupid *name*. From the beginning she'd known that Reno probably wasn't his real name, but after a while she'd stopped thinking about it. It hadn't seemed important, and eventually she'd forgotten about it completely.

No! She hadn't lost him, what was she thinking of? He'd call, of course. He'd call Nancy, looking for her. He probably already had called. She had to find a telephone.

Jenna shook back her hair, brushed tear traces from her cheeks and reached for the ignition.

"Well, howdy, stranger, look what the storm blew in!" Twyla cracked as Nate plowed through the kitchen on the way to his office. When he didn't slam the door, she followed him and stood in the doorway with her arms folded, watching him tear into the piles of debris on his desk. "Hon," she observed after a moment, "you look like you just lost your best friend."

"Not if I have anything to say about it," Nate muttered through his teeth as he riffled through a notebook and then tossed it aside.

Twyla grabbed for a stack of breeding records just as they were about to slide off onto the floor. Nate glanced at her. "You been cleaning up in here?"

"Hell no, I value my life. What in the world are you looking for?"

"Nothing. Just a little piece of paper with some numbers on it. It's a license number. You seen it?"

Twyla just snorted. She lit up a cigarette, waved out the match and elbowed Nate aside. "Here, you aren't going to find anything that way. You're just making a mess."

Nate scowled at her. "Yeah? Well give me a hand, then. And while you're at it, give me one of those cigarettes, will you?"

"What are you doing? You don't smoke. And you aren't goin' to start, either."

"What are you, my mother?" Nate snarled. "Give me the goddam cigarette."

Twyla looked at him for a minute or two, then shook out another cigarette, lit it and handed it to him without a word. Nate hadn't smoked since the minors, and his first drag

burned all the way down to the bottom of his lungs. It didn't
hurt half as bad as he'd been hurting all day anyway. After
a long, slow exhalation he looked at Twyla and muttered,
"Thanks." She just shrugged. He took a couple more puffs
on the cigarette and leaned back in his chair with a sigh.
"Ah, shoot—how are things? Vaccinating go okay? Anything been happening around here I should know about?"

"Naw," Twyla said, "everything's fine. Here—" She
held up a piece of notebook paper. "This what you're
lookin' for?"

Nate snatched it out of her hand, stared at it then leaned
back in his chair again and closed his eyes.

Jenna's license-plate number. He hadn't lost it, and he
wasn't going to lose her. Not without a fight. He'd waited
too long to find her in the first place. And he'd find her
again, no matter how long it took.

Jenna pulled off into the first gas station she came to that
had a pay phone. Her heart was pounding and her knees
were weak as she walked to the booth; her hands shook as
she dialed. The receiver felt slippery in her hand.

She let it ring six times before she remembered that Nancy
wouldn't be there. She'd have been at the library all day, so
even if Reno had called, she wouldn't have been there to
take it. She thought about calling Nancy at work—but to
what purpose? There was nothing she could tell her, nothing at all.

Finally, in the bleak loneliness of the telephone booth,
Jenna knew she had no choice but to accept temporary de-
feat. She couldn't do anything until Nancy heard from
Reno. And in the meantime, she'd made a bargain. She'd
promised Jack Remington a show in two weeks time and she
had to keep her end of the bargain because she was going to
find Reno again, and when she did, she intended to hold
Jack to his promise. For the next two weeks, at least, she'd
sold her soul to the Remington Galleries.

On the way home to Los Angeles she crossed the high
arching bridge that spanned the gorge where the Old Coach

Station Inn nestled in timeless purple shadows. It had been almost the same time of day, she remembered, when she'd taken that turnoff, less than a week ago. A lifetime ago.

It seemed unreal to her now, just a distant fantasy. Like Camelot.

"Remington Gallery, may I help you?" said the clear, young voice on the telephone.

"Well, I'm not sure," Nate said, and paused to clear his throat. His heart was hammering like he'd just executed a suicide squeeze play in the bottom of the ninth inning. "Is, ummm...is Jenna there, by any chance?"

"Oh, I'm sorry," the voice responded promptly, "Miss McBride is busy getting ready for the opening of her new show this evening. Were you interested in the Camelot Series?"

"Camelot Series...yes, I sure am," Nate said heartily; he always had been pretty good at thinking on his feet. "You say that's opening tonight?"

"Tonight's showing is private, invitation only, I'm afraid. The show opens to the public tomorrow. The gallery opens at noon, if you'd like—"

"Listen, tell me this," Nate said in his best Texas drawl. "How would I go about gettin' an invitation to tonight's showing? I've got a little money I'd like to invest, and I have a special interest in Miss McBride—in her work, that is. I'd kind of like to have first crack at it, if you know what I mean."

"Well, I don't know...if you'll give me your name, perhaps I can speak to Mr. Remington."

"I'd appreciate it. This is Nathan Wells. Anything you can do—"

"Nathan Wells? *Nate* Wells? You mean—Oh my God!" The receptionist's voice lost its professional decorum completely and suddenly became human, feminine, excited and very young. "Mr. Wells—you have no idea what a thrill this is. My brother used to have a poster of you on his bedroom wall! When I was in seventh grade I was practically in love

with you. Oh, God, I know I'm probably embarrassing
you—listen, there's no problem about tonight. I mean—I'm
putting your name on the guest list right now. Just tell
whoever's at the door and they'll check you off."

"Well," Nate said, "that's sure nice of you."

"Oh—no problem. My pleasure. I just hope I get a
chance to meet you in person."

"I'm lookin' forward to it. And thanks very much...."

"Carla."

"Thanks, Carla. You've been a big help. See you tonight, then."

"Yeah.... Oh—Mr. Wells, I almost forgot," Carla said,
recovering her poise in the nick of time. "The reception—
it's black tie."

Nate sighed, grimacing at the telephone. "Thanks for
tellin' me." Terrific, he thought. Evening clothes. And the
plane was being overhauled and Tom and Twyla were taking the car to San Luis for a night on the town. That left him
with either the bike or the Bronco.

The low murmur of sound in the gallery's main hall was
like the refrain of an old familiar song to Jenna. Along with
the smell—a mixture of champagne, expensive cologne and
fresh-cut flowers—it brought back memories of so many
other openings, so many other receptions, so many other
beautiful, rich or famous people.

She was nervous, of course, not to mention tense, keyed-
up, and physically exhausted, but she hid it well. After all,
she'd been born to this. She'd attended her first formal reception at the age of six, in a black velvet dress with white
satin bows and a white satin bow in her hair.... She could
almost see her parents as they'd looked then, their two heads
close together, her father's dark, her mother's blond, the
center of an adoring group of admirers, like twin suns surrounded by lesser bodies. Ian and Audrey McBride, the
fairest of the fair....

A wave of loneliness swept over her, catching her by surprise. She missed her parents and she missed Reno, and all

she wanted was for this night to be over so she could get back to the only thing that mattered to her now—finding him. To forestall the tears she could feel pricking at the backs of her eyelids, she snagged a glass of champagne from a passing waiter and moved to the foot of the stairs, sipping as she went.

The evening's host hadn't made his appearance yet, but he was due at any moment. Jack Remington liked to wait until he had a full house. Then he'd come down those stairs, as Jenna had seen him do so many times...graceful and unhurried, looking impossibly gorgeous, elegant and distinguished in his impeccably cut dinner jacket and immaculately groomed silver hair, making everyone else in the room, including her, look frumpy and clumsy by comparison.

Annoyed that Jack Remington could still have that effect on her, Jenna hid a sardonic smile with her champagne glass. No, she didn't look frumpy—her green satin gown, by a well-known designer, was suitably expensive and fit her like a glove. She'd pulled one side of her hair back and pinned it with a diamond clip, and the emerald-and-diamond earrings her parents had given her for her eighteenth birthday were in her ears. She knew she was as elegantly turned out as it was possible for someone so milkmaid wholesome to be...but she couldn't resist turning, nevertheless, to check her reflection in the darkened windows just beyond the stairs.

She looked...and went ice cold with shock. The fingers that held the champagne glass lost all feeling. She turned reflexively back toward the stairs, trying to reject what she'd seen in the glass, but it was too late. At the precise moment that Jack Remington started down the stairs, the champagne glass slipped from Jenna's nerveless hand and shattered on the marble floor.

All sound and motion in the hall ceased, and then resumed at a different level—curious, inquisitive, concerned. A look of annoyance crossed Jack's face and was almost instantly replaced by one of solicitude. Jenna

watched him come toward her down the stairs, but it was as
if he were moving in slow motion. *She* was moving in slow
motion. She wanted to turn and look, but...

"Jenna, are you all right?" Jack was beside her, his hand
on her elbow. She nodded and murmured something—an
explanation or apology. Satisfied, he moved away from her,
efficiently summoning waiters, intercepting and reassuring
concerned patrons.

Left on her own, Jenna pivoted slowly, feeling as if her
joints had rusted. "Reno," she said.   A different Reno.
Reno in evening clothes was a breathtaking sight; beside
him, Jack Remington's flawless elegance seemed pale and
two-dimensional, like an image on celluloid. Reno's hair
was as windblown as ever; his jacket was unbuttoned and his
tie askew, giving him a slightly rakish look, like a riverboat
gambler. Even in a tuxedo he looked raw, tough and dangerous. And angry. That was the real difference, Jenna
thought, trembling inside. Reno was angry.

"Hello, Gingerbread Lady." He smiled, not the slow,
sweet smile she loved, but something else—cold, cynical, a
bit off-center. His lion's rumble stirred her auditory nerves
like fingers stroking a cat's fur the wrong way.

She opened her mouth to respond, but before she could
Jack was there with a proprietary hand on her shoulder, in-
quiring about her welfare, handing her a napkin. Resisting
an urge to shake off his touch, Jenna assured him irritably
that she was fine and that the damage to her dress was min-
imal. He reached across her shoulder to shake Reno's hand.

"I don't believe I've met you. I'm Jack Remington."

Reno's eyes narrowed slightly, but he accepted the hand-
shake and muttered, "Nate Wells."

Jenna felt like a spectator caught right in the middle of a
tennis match.

"Ah yes, Mr. Wells." Jack's voice was smooth and cool
as glass. "I'm glad you could make it. It seems my receptionist is a big fan of yours. Maybe we can find something
around here for you to autograph for her, if you wouldn't
mind. It would make her day." Nate muttered something

noncommittal. Jack showed his teeth in a smile and squeezed Jenna's shoulders. "Well, I see you've met our lovely artist. What do you think of the Camelot Series, Mr. Wells?"

"Haven't seen it yet." Nate's jaws felt as if they could crush rocks.

"No? Well, in that case—Jenna, why don't you show Mr. Wells around while I go and charm the critics. Nice meeting you, Nate." He shook Nate's hand again and moved off, after giving Jenna's shoulders one more squeeze.

Silence settled around them, thick and insulating, shimmering with tension and suppressed emotions. For a long time they just looked at each other, until finally Nate coughed and said, "Well, Jenna McBride..."

Jenna gave a little pain-filled laugh. "Nathan Wells?" She looked away, swallowing repeatedly, and after a moment managed to say, "Do you want me to show you around?"

Nate growled, "I didn't come to see your paintings. I came to see you."

She didn't say anything. He noticed that she seemed pale, and that her eyes were shadowed, so he tried to hold off his feelings, to hold on to his anger. "That's him, isn't it?" he said sardonically, jerking his head toward Remington. "The guy who wouldn't touch you. I see you seem to have worked out your differences."

Jenna turned, if possible, even paler. "What do you mean?"

Nate shrugged...made himself smile. "Well, darlin', he doesn't seem to have any trouble touching you now. Can't keep his hands off of you. So—I guess you got what you wanted." He turned away from her then because he just couldn't bear to look at her any longer. If he went on looking at her he'd have to either strangle her or take her in his arms. Hell, maybe he'd just throw her over his shoulder and carry her out of this place....

"It's not what you think," she said faintly.

"Yeah?" He turned to look at her one more time. "You came back to him, didn't you?"

"Yes, but—" He heard her catch her breath. "Where are you going?"

He was leaving, only because he'd finally had all he could take. But the panic in her voice tugged at him like an anchor, so he stopped reluctantly, took a breath and squared his shoulders. "Look..." His voice felt like he'd swallowed gravel, but he kept on going. "I came just to see how you were, why you'd left. I see things seem to be working out for you, so now I'm goin' home. That's all." He started walking again, and this time when she called his name he didn't stop.

"Reno! Please..." Forgetting everything, ignoring everyone, Jenna ran after him, through the glass double doors and out onto the sidewalk. Somehow, she wasn't even surprised to see the big black motorcycle parked at the curb, in the space reserved for valet parking. "Reno, wait!" She was desperate to stop him, to make him understand. "It's not what you think at all. I only came back because of you."

He'd already straddled the bike and had one foot on the starter, but when she said that, he sat back and waited for her to come to him. "Mind explainin'?" he said softly, dangerously.

Jenna's heart trembled in her chest. "It was a business arrangement," she said rapidly. "I made a deal with Jack. I agreed to do this show if he—"

"Yeah?"

She took a deep breath. "If he'd agree to show your sculpture—here, in the gallery."

She waited but he didn't say anything for a long time, just looked at her with eyes like black holes. At last he shook his head and let his breath out with a soft wondering hiss. "And that's why you left me without a word and came back here to him?" She nodded. He looked down at his hands, fiddling restlessly with the handlebar grips, and swore quietly under his breath.   "Jenna." His voice was painful to hear. The look on his face frightened her because she realized then how badly she'd hurt him. "Don't you think you should have asked me if that's what I wanted? You think this is what I want?" He waved his arm, taking in the gallery with its glass facade, crystal chandeliers and banks of ferns and flowers, the lights of Wilshire and the whole city beyond. "Lady, I've had this. I've had fame, more than you can possibly imagine, and believe me, it's not what it's cracked up to be. I don't need to have my stuff in some fancy gallery, damn it! What I wanted—all I wanted—was *you.*"

"But that's—" Jenna took a step toward him. He held up a hand, stopping her in her tracks.

"I talked to your friend Nancy," he said softly. "She told me about your little game . . . how it wasn't supposed to be anything serious." His laugh had a hollow sound. "You should have told me that, darlin'. I'd have played along. Hell, I'm good at games. I spent most of my life playing games." All at once his voice sounded sad. "And I'm damn tired of games, Jenna. I'm not some kind of fantasy—black knight or whatever you happen to make me out to be—I'm just a man, that's all. And what I want is to be with you, to share my life with you, on a permanent, full-time basis. I want to go to bed with you every night and wake up with you every morning, eat my meals with you, make babies with you. That's reality, darlin'. That's the real thing. And that's what I want."

He kicked the starter and the big bike roared to life. Nate turned his head to look at her one more time. "If you can't handle that," he said, raising his voice just enough so she could hear him above the racket of the Harley's engine, "then stay right here—quit playin' games with my life!"

He roared away down the street, leaving Jenna standing there like a stone column on the sidewalk.

A man wearing a white cowboy hat and lizard-skin cowboy boots with his tuxedo was just getting out of a limo at the curb. "Hey," he said to Jenna, grinning like a schoolboy, "do you know who that was? That was Nate Wells! Hell of a ballplayer—do you know, I've seen him pitch!"

"Yes," Jenna murmured as her heart began to beat again, as her lungs filled with air, as wonder exploded through her consciousness and joy ran through her like crystal rivers. "Yes," she said, hugging herself and beginning to shake in spite of it, laughing and crying at the same time. "Oh, yes, so have I...."

It was an hour past sunup by the time Jenna got to the valley. She'd left the gallery some time after midnight and headed straight up the coast without going home or changing her clothes, but fatigue had finally caught up with her on the Pacific Coast Highway and she'd had to pull into a truck stop for a fifteen-minute nap. The sun woke her. After a cup of coffee in the truck stop café—and a lot of strange looks—she was on her way again, still wearing her green satin dress, high heeled shoes and her emerald-and-diamond earrings.

She didn't have any trouble at all finding the ranch the second time, but just to make sure, she stopped at the foot of the lane, rolled down her window and called to a very tall young black man with a cast on his leg, who was leaning on crutches, painting the white rail fence with a power sprayer.

"Excuse me—is this Nathan Wells's ranch?"

The boy regarded her with suspicion for a moment, then pointed with the sprayer nozzle. "That's the place," he said in a thick ghetto drawl, "right up there."

"Thanks," Jenna called, giving him a radiant smile.

When Jenna stopped her car in front of the ranch house, she didn't see the dogs. It wouldn't have made any difference if she had. This time nothing was going to stop her. She marched up the steps to the porch and knocked on the door, and when the thin, redhaired woman answered, Jenna announced forthrightly, "Hi, I'm Jenna McBride. Is Nate—is Mr. Wells in?"

"No, he's not," the woman rasped, drying her hands on a dishtowel and regarding Jenna with a frown. "Wait, aren't you the one—"

"He's up at his cabin."

Jenna turned around. The bow-legged man was coming across the yard, leading a horse by the reins, all four dogs trotting at his heels.

"You must be Jenna," he said, holding out his hand. "I'm Tom, and this here's my wife, Twyla. Nate just left. He said you might be along. Said if you showed up, to tell you that's where he'd be."

"Thank you," Jenna said, breathlessly shaking the weathered hand, quelling an urge to throw her arms around the man and hug him. "Can you please give me directions? I'm not sure I can find my way."

Tom shook his head. "Only way to get there is on that bike, or horseback. I'd be happy to take you, but I don't think you're dressed for it. Twyla could probably find you some clothe—"

"On...a horse?" Jenna asked, regarding the animal with horror. She'd vowed nothing would keep her from finding Reno, but... "I've never been on a horse in my life!"

Tom shrugged and scratched his head. "Well..."

All four dogs suddenly sat up, ears alert and quivering, then abruptly took off down the narrow dirt road. A second or two later, Jenna heard it, too. The throbbing of a powerful engine.

And then somehow she was standing in the road, her heart beating so hard her whole body rocked with it, breathing in shallow sips, watching the bike and its black-jacketed rider come over the hill. He pulled up and stopped a few yards away from her, engine idling. Tension screamed inside her head; she doubted her legs would hold her. She'd come this far on sheer courage, but she'd about exhausted her supply. What would he say to her? Would he ever forgive her? She didn't even know if he still wanted her.

"I thought you'd gone," Tom said mildly.

"Well," Nate drawled, never taking his eyes from Jenna's face, "I just had a feeling I should come back."

Jenna swallowed hard, but still could only whisper. "I always knew you were a wizard."

"What?" Nate's eyes narrowed.

She held out her hands. "I'm sorry." Her voice broke; her whole body was shaking. "I have an imagination. I can't help it, it's just a part of me. It's who I am."

Nate's eyes stabbed at her, searching the very depths of her soul. Tension sang like clouds of mosquitoes in the air between them, building and building until she thought she might suffocate from it. Until at last he nodded.

"As long as you know what's real and what's not." It was his wooly voice, scratchy... warm.

"I know," Jenna whispered.

There was another pause, a shorter one this time, and then Nate jerked his head in that imperious way of his and said, low in his throat, "Hey—come 'ere."

She moved to him on unsteady legs.

"Hop on," he growled, holding out his hand. "I'll give you a ride."

"I don't think I'm dressed for it," Jenna said, shaking so hard she could barely stand.

Nate's slow, sweet smile broke over his face like a sunrise. "Sure you are," he drawled. "If you don't mind showin' a little leg."

Laughter rose in Jenna's throat. She caught her breath, and her lower lip between her teeth. "Atta girl," Nate said softly. His eyes began to glow like coals as he watched her hike her green satin gown up to her hips.

"Wait!" Breathless and laughing, she bent over, pulled off her shoes and tossed them over her shoulder. Then she straddled the seat as if she'd been born to it and wrapped her arms around Nate's body.

"Hold on!" he shouted as he gunned the bike's engine, and she did, as hard as she dared, as though she would never, ever let go.

She went with him, riding as if her body and his were one and the same, while the wind raked her hair back and blew his against her face. She rode with him over bumpy roads and through fields of wildflowers, until at last the bike dropped down into the gully, rumbled across the creek on the wooden bridge, surged up and over the bank on the far side and came to a stop in front of the cabin.

Nate dismounted, dragged her roughly from the saddle and into his arms, carried her across the porch and kicked open the cabin door. In the doorway he stopped and looked down at her, his eyes like probes.

"You'd better be damn sure," he growled.

"I am," Jenna said with absolute certainty. "I love you."

"In that case," he said in a breaking whisper, just before his mouth covered hers, "Gingerbread Lady... welcome home."

* * * * *

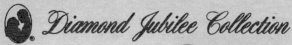

SILHOUETTE·INTIMATE·MOMENTS®

**Premiering in September,
a captivating new cover
for Silhouette's most adventurous
series!**

Every month, Silhouette Intimate Moments sweeps
you away with four dramatic love stories rich in
passion. Silhouette Intimate Moments presents
love at its most romantic, where life is exciting
and dreams do come true.

**Look for the new cover next month,
wherever you buy Silhouette® books.**

2IMNC-1

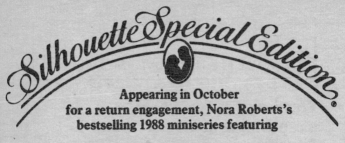

Appearing in October
for a return engagement, Nora Roberts's
bestselling 1988 miniseries featuring

THE O'HURLEYS!
Nora Roberts

Book 1 **THE LAST HONEST WOMAN** *Abby's Story*
Book 2 **DANCE TO THE PIPER** *Maddy's Story*
Book 3 **SKIN DEEP** *Chantel's Story*

And making his debut in a brand-new title, a very special
leading man . . . Trace O'Hurley!

Book 4 **WITHOUT A TRACE** *Trace's Tale*

In 1988, Nora Roberts introduced THE O'HURLEYS!—a close-knit
family of entertainers whose early travels spanned the country. The
beautiful triplet sisters and their mysterious brother each experience
the triumphant joy and passion only true love can bring, in four books
you will remember long after the last pages are turned.

Don't miss this captivating miniseries in October—a special collec-
tor's edition available wherever paperbacks are sold.

Double your reading pleasure this fall with two Award of Excellence titles written by two of your favorite authors.

Available in September

DUNCAN'S BRIDE
by Linda Howard
Silhouette Intimate Moments #349

Mail-order bride Madelyn Patterson was nothing like what Reese Duncan expected—and everything he needed.

Available in October

THE COWBOY'S LADY
by Debbie Macomber
Silhouette Special Edition #626

The Montana cowboy wanted a little lady at his beck and call—the "lady" in question saw things differently....

These titles have been selected to receive a special laurel—the Award of Excellence. Look for the distinctive emblem on the cover. It lets you know there's something truly wonderful inside!   DUN-1